GRAVITY
JOURNAL

GRAVITY JOURNAL

Gail Sidonie Sobat

GREAT PLAINS
PUBLICATIONS

Copyright © 2008 Gail Sidonie Sobat
5th printing

Great Plains Teen Fiction
(an imprint of Great Plains Publications)
233 Garfield Street S
Winnipeg, MB R3G 2M1
www.greatplains.mb.ca

All rights reserved. No part of this publication may be reproduced or transmitted in any form or in any means, or stored in a database and retrieval system, without the prior written permission of Great Plains Publications, or, in the case of photocopying or other reprographic copying, a license from Access Copyright (Canadian Copyright Licensing Agency), 1 Yonge Street, Suite 1900, Toronto, Ontario, Canada, M5E 1E5.

Great Plains Publications gratefully acknowledges the financial support provided for its publishing program by the Government of Canada through the Canada Book Fund; the Canada Council for the Arts; the Province of Manitoba through the Book Publishing Tax Credit and the Book Publisher Marketing Assistance Program; and the Manitoba Arts Council.

Design & Typography by Relish New Brand Experience
Printed in Canada by Friesens

Library and Archives Canada Cataloguing in Publication

Sobat, Gail Sidonie
Gravity Journal / Gail Sidonie Sobat.

ISBN 978-1-894283-78-6

    I. Title.

PS8587.O23G73 2008   jC813'.6   C2008-900494-9

The lyrics to "Walk Away" by Tom Barlow are used with the artist's kind permission.

ACKNOWLEDGEMENTS

So many people contributed to the making of this novel. Thank you to Duane Stewart, beloved mentor, whose careful eyes and honest pen continue to challenge and guide me. Thanks to Sara Kapler, M.A., R.Psych, who shared her psychological and readerly expertise with me about the manuscript. Thanks to Jen Rae who granted me permission and who gave me guidance, and because of whom I wisely no longer permit weigh scales in my life. Thanks to my wonderful colleagues at the hospital school and especially, my friend, Frank Elliott who daily is an exemplar of excellent teaching seasoned with compassion. Thanks to my editor/publisher Gregg Shilliday — you're simply the best!

I cannot thank all the students by name whose lives have touched mine, or express adequately how they have inspired me with their courage and strength. But special thanks go to Joanne Kerr (I owe you for that story — you know the one), Amelia Carroll, Brittany Wesley, Nathan Wong, Celeste Hernandez, Stephanie Ewasiuk, Janelle Kulak, Michelle Johnson, Marika Pagotto, Kory Ring, Christina Sikora, Christina Kotylak, Danielle McDonald, Kaylee Netterfield, Anna Wehrfritz-Hanson, Sherise Schlaht, Lauren Seal, Desiree Chambers and many others — you know who you are and what you mean to me.

Thanks finally to my mother — you saved my life on so many levels —and to Geoff, as always, for supporting and nurturing girls and women, especially this one, in your life.

For Desiree Chambers
I hold you in the light and Jen Rae, for yours.

This is a work of fiction. Any resemblance to actual persons, living or dead, is entirely coincidental.

First Words

New journal. New day. Supposed to be. And didn't it all begin so well?

In the anals (sic) of King Edward Academy of the Arts, the sick girl approaches her very own locker. An ironic Number 13. And some thoughtful one has taped to it a huge photograph. Maybe taken at Aushwitz or Buchenwald or some more recent site of atrocity. A corpse. Emaciated. Skeleton poking through withered flesh. Wide staring eyeballs in shrunken sockets.

The sick girl stands there staring. The rigor mortis of the cadaver has become her own.

Underneath the photo is a name. Anise.

My name is Anise, she remembers.

And slips silently to the cold floor.

Chapter one

Blood, bright and satisfying, oozed from the cut on her upper forearm. Such a straight line. Neat and orderly next the other scars. Horizontal ladder rungs up her arm. Each the same length and width. Each a marker.

Anise watched the tiny rivulet trickle down to her wrist and onto the bathroom countertop. Her arm incarnadine. She liked that word: incarnadine. It reminded her of Macbeth and Lady Macbeth trying to wash their hands clean of blood. Of guilt. Of shame. Lady Macbeth was Anise's favourite character in Shakespeare. Well, of all five plays she'd ever read.

> Today:
> What hands are here? Ha! they pluck out mine eyes.
> Will all great Neptune's ocean wash this blood
> Clean from my hand? No, this my hand will rather
> The multitudinous seas incarnadine
> Making the green one red.

She looked at the blood pooling on the white counter. She could take a pin and write her name.

Anise. Anise. Ani...

Slumping down on the floor, she looked at her arm. Pale with tiny blue veins. She balanced her elbow on her knee to watch the blood trickle downwards. Gravity. Gravity pulls the blood towards the earth.

Gravity. Grave. Gravitas.

Anise liked the link between those words.

She concentrated on the cut and gave her arm a little squeeze to increase the bloodflow. Doesn't hurt. Doesn't hurt.

Tried to will her mind from the events of the day. The incident with her locker at school. The argument, bitter and hateful, with the loathsome female parent. The lousy mark on her math exam. Her weight.

Anise watched the blood calmly and let the hurt of the wound fill her up.

Suicide Intervention Alert says:

Self-harm is defined as a deliberate and often repetitive destruction or alteration of one's own body tissue, without suicidal intent (adapted from Favazza, 1987 & 1989, and Walsh & Rosen, 1988). Many terms have been used to describe this behaviour including self-harm, self-injury, self-mutilation, self-inflicted violence, auto-aggression, and parasuicide.

Someone rapped on the bathroom door.

"Yeah, what?" Anise grabbed a towel, threw it hastily over the bloody counter. Took another and wrapped the soft cotton about her arm. Steeled herself.

"Hey, Licorice-breath, that you?"

"Yeah," Anise whispered to her brother, releasing her tight shoulders.

"Lemme in. I gotta take a whiz."

"Give me a minute, will you?" Anise ran the cold tap and worked at the red pool, wiping the white arborite clean. She pulled the sleeve of her pajama top down over the hand towel still wrapped around her arm.

"Geez, Anise! Hurry up, will you!"

Anise snapped her journal shut, cracked the door open. "Are the units awake?"

"Nope. Outta my way."

Anise left the washroom and pressed her back against the adjacent wall, hugging her notebook to her chest. She stared at the closed door at the opposite end of the long hallway. Her parents took sleeping pills. Faithfully. They seldom stirred before 4:30 am. How long had she been in the bathroom? She'd left her room at around 1 am.

"Hey, Marcel! What time's it?" She could hear a steady stream from behind the door.

"After 3." He flushed and opened the door, light spilling into the hallway gloom. "How come you're up?"

"How come you're home so flippin' late?"

Marcel grinned. "In a word? Alana."

Anise grimaced. She detested Marcel's girlfriend. Lithe model bitch. Shallow. Everything Anise hated in girls. And everything Marcel lusted after.

They spoke in undertones.

"Really, 'Nise. Can't you sleep?"

"No."

"Want me to snag some of the parental meds?"

"Don't you think I'm on enough meds, already, Mars?"

"Is there such a thing?"

She winced. Marcel liked his drugs. X. Acid. Pills. She worried he'd been experimenting with crystal meth. "Shut up. I don't need anything. It's just... you know. I'm going back tomorrow."

"Oh yeah. I forgot."

Marcel followed her into her room. The lava lamp turned somersaults on her bedside table. Music throbbed through the headphones discarded on the rumpled duvet. They stepped over the mounds of clothing and flopped down on the floor beside the half-filled suitcase.

"I'm freezing." Anise was shaking visibly, despite her thick flannel pjs.

"It's warm in here. Stuffy. Here, Anise..." Marcel grabbed the duvet and tucked it around his sister's slight shoulders.

"Thanks."

They listened to Our Lady Peace coming through in miniature stereo from the headphones.

"Hey, Allsorts. What's the volume at? 35? What would the units do if I just unplugged the jack of the phones for a minute?" Marcel reached towards the Sony.

"Mars! Don't!" She grabbed his arm and they struggled briefly, laughing. Marcel gave in.

"They wouldn't even notice is my guess."

"Prob'ly not, Allsorts, prob'ly not." He swept his hand through his hair and returned her grin. "Geez, Anise. There's something I rarely see anymore."

"What?"

"You smiling."

"So what's to smile about?"

"I dunno. Getting laid. Partying."

Anise snorted. "You're mistaking your aspirations for my miserable life."

Marcel looked away, then glanced at her journal. "Anything new for me?"

His sister opened the black cover with a pale, shaking hand. "I'm working on an ode."

"Dead white guys write odes, Anise. You're neither."
"Yet."
"Shut up with that, ok! Read."
She flipped through the pages. Cleared her throat:

Ode to Alana

O, creature vexing awesome
I envy thee thy tresses golden
Legs limber lithesome long
Breasts gargantuan yet falsely, too
Thy skin fair, orbs bluely luminescent
Thy breathing sweetly shallow
And mind at a loss for words intelligible
And yet the sweet shepherd harkens
To your siren call
Alas, the poor shepherd, dupe and clown
In her poison'd embrace all fools must drown

"Ha, ha. Very funny. Doesn't matter if you like her, sis. She digs me!" Marcel yawned like a lion. "Time for my beauty rest." He paused before her bureau mirror, gazed admiringly at his reflection. "Although, it's true I don't need much at that. Good poem, though, little sister. You're a riot. G'night."

"Marcel?"

"Huh?"

"Are you coming with us tomorrow?"

"Where?"

"To the hospital, stupid. When they commit, I mean, admit me."

"Sure, Allsorts. I'll be there." Marcel closed the door behind him.

Anise felt very weak suddenly. Thought she might keel over. She pulled herself and the duvet onto the bed.

A soft knock and Marcel's beautiful head reappeared, framed by her doorway. "Hey, Anise. Do something for me, will ya?"

"What, Mars?"

"Get better this time, ok."

"I'll think about it."

Marcel...boy wonder. Enfant terrible. Athlete. Don Juan. Smartass. Lazyass. Popular. Destined for stardom. Risk-taker. Idiot. Loser. Bad taste in women. Only person who truly loves me.

Anise clicked off the lights and tried not to dream.

Chapter two

4-Psych. O-Ward. The dreaded ward of the Eliza Petraclark Memorial Hospital. Better known as 4-Psych-O. Or for psychos. All the inmates called it that. Whichever suit named it, had obviously missed the irony. But the inmates and the staff didn't. 4-Psych-O. Where all the loonies go once they fly off the Canadian dollar coin.

Anise's mood was dark as the liner around her eyes. She hated 4-Psych-O. But not as much as she hated 4-Psych-O, Room 111, where she was seated now in Dr. Zeplin's boring office that smelled of old. Old books. Old papers. Old coffee scorching on the burner. Old anemic plants clawing at the windows for a breath. Or to break out.

"It's just about her one-year anniversary since her last stay here," the loathsome female parent began. "We thought she'd be over this by now. But apparently not."

"Yes, the nurses have noted a deterioration over the past dozen weeks or so," Dr. Z nodded agreeably, peering at the thick file that was the sum of Anise's sick life.

"Do you think this time she'll be cured, Doctor?" The witless male parent seldom cracked a comment.

"We hesitate to use the word cure. And it's entirely up to Anise, of course."

At the mention of her name, Anise slouched down deeper in her chair. All of this was so tiring. And she was so very tired already. Couldn't they all just leave her alone? Let her slip away unnoticed. No one would notice if she just...

"Can she at least have a better roommate than last time?"

Marcel's voice started Anise. She glanced over at him, leaning in the corner, looking uncomfortable. Unhappy.

"Marcel!" Loathed scolded.

"Mom, you know that half-witch was not good for Anise. She needs someone her own age. Someone halfways intelligent. Or she'll go..."

Stark raving mad? Anise thought. Too late, bro. Anise smiled blandly at his efforts. Already crazy. That's why I'm here, isn't it? She closed her eyes...

...and drifted up and out of her disgusting body. So light and free. Weightless. Above the heads of the others. Out the door and away. Beyond the building. Up. Light as a breath of cloud. Liberated.

From far away a voice. A woman's voice.

"Anise."

"Anise!"

Her eyes flicked open.

"Anise!! Dr. Zeplin is talking to you. He wants you to go with the nurse."

Anise tried to recognize the speaker. Yes. The loathsome female parent. She remembered now. 4-Psych-O. Hell. She was back in hell. Anise rose shakily from the chair. Marcel reached to steady her. The nurse at the door took over.

"Come on, Anise. Time for the scale. Then maybe we'll get you something to drink."

Anise walked down the long corridor towards the scale. She wanted to run away. It had been weeks since she'd weighed herself. The other girls stared out from their rooms or from the hallway sofas at her. Anise knew they all despised her, the way she would despise new admits in the weeks to come. She slipped off her shoes and stepped onto the scale.

"How tall are you, Anise?"

"Um. 5'9."

"Ok. Let's see now." The nurse's voice was sickeningly cheery. Anise glanced at her nametag. Of course, her name would be Felicity. Anise would have laughed if she'd had the energy. Nothing mattered. Now that they were locking her up, about to force her to eat. To gain weight. To get fat.

"So. Today you weigh 44 kg."

Shit. The ugly truth. Anise was hoping for 40 kg. Now that she was here, in 4-Psych-O, they'd never let her reach the perfect goal. She wished she could be alone. In her own room. In the bathroom. Anywhere else.

"I'll show you your room, Anise. Room 12. You'll be sharing with Zoe."

"Hi." A listless form in silhouette against the window barely turned her head towards Anise.

"Zoe's having a rough day." Nurse Felicity chirruped so that Anise wanted to hit her.

At that moment, Marcel's voice stopped her from doing violence. "Hey, Licorice-breath. Here's your stuff." He walked in and plopped two suitcases on the neatly-made, sterile bed.

"Good then, Anise. Make yourself at home." Felicity smiled emptily at Marcel and left the room.

Her brother nodded over at the other room occupant. Glanced at the posters on the wall. "Once you get some pictures up and your own bedding, Nise, it'll look better. You've got your iPod, so you've got your tunes. And I got you a gift."

"What?"

He pulled the curtains around her bed for a semblance of privacy. Then handed her a brightly coloured gift bag, one she recognized from a birthday gift she'd given him. "Call it an early b-day present. But don't show the units."

Anise unfolded the tissue paper around a tiny licorice coloured cellphone. "Marcel, they don't let us have these in here. And the units confiscated mine. What are you doing?" Anise hissed.

"Shhhh, stupid. It's small. Easily concealed. It's on my account. Use it with discretion and no one will be the wiser. That way we can always be in touch. If you need me and stuff."

Anise hugged her brother, wanting never to let go.

Their parents walked in on them, announcing their arrival with a flourish of the bed curtain. Marcel managed to secrete the phone under the pillow.

"Well, Anise. We're finished with the doctor. Is there anything else you need right now?" the loathed one spoke.

"Nope."

Her mother peered at her. Sighing, she turned to go. "Ok, then. Take care of yourself. Get better. And we'll see you soon, dear."

"Bye for now, Nise. You'll be home in no time." Her father, always so good with words.

"See ya, Allsorts."

No, Marcel. Not you. Stay. Please don't leave me here. Anise's thoughts spilled over each other in a panic. "Bye."

Marcel turned hurriedly away. She could see he was choked. Loathed and Witless left behind him.

Anise wished she could cry.

Instead, she reached for the trash can and stuck her finger down her throat.

Chapter three

D r. Zeplin the archfiend has diagnosed me. Apparently, I'm anorexic—binge eating/purging type—and, just for added fun, I present symptoms of Major Depressive Disorder. Well, what news! Same old, same old. Same thing last year. So how much are they going to help me this year?

> *Anorexia Nervosa: a combination of symptoms including amenorrhea, extreme emaciation, hypothermia, over-activity and lack of appetite; medical term first coined by Sir William Gull.*
>
> *All of us here on 4-Psych-O thank you, Sir William, Sir Gull.*
>
> *Gull: 1594. [Middle English] 1. A credulous person; a dupe, simpleton, fool. 2. A trick, deception, fraud; a false report - 1668. 3. slang. A trickster, cheat 1700. (Oxford English Dictionary)*
>
> *Amenorrhea: 1804. [modern Latin from Greek - month + flowing.] Medical. Absence or suppression of the menstrual discharge. (OED)*

My last period... hmmm, let's see. It's January, so maybe last summer?

Anise looked away from her journal and the open tome of the *Oxford English Dictionary*, with its well-thumbed pages, beside her on her bed. Zoe was busy at work on her project for Bio 30. A lengthy research paper, since she couldn't attend regular classes. Zoe's thinning hair fell forward as she scribbled in her notebook. She concentrated keenly, a pen grasped so tightly in her hand that her knuckles were white.

"How's it goin', Zo'?"

Her roommate turned a joyless face towards Anise.

"I don't think I'm doing very well, Anise. I think I'm going to get a lousy mark."

"Zoe, you're doing great. Just keep the faith and keep going." Anise almost choked on her own words, rehearsed from last week's group therapy session. But she wanted to be supportive of Zoe. That, at least, was real.

"Hi Anise. Hi Zoe," a cheery voice sang at the door. Both looked at the frail form grinning in at them. Ivana, almost thirty, had been in and out of the program and 4-Psych-O for going on seven years, sick for maybe ten.

"How're you both doin'?"

"Swell." Anise's flat tone did nothing to dampen the woman's enthusiasm.

"Keep on keepin' on!" Anise winced at how familiar the refrain sounded to that she'd offered Zoe only a moment before. She hoped her voice hadn't sounded as hollow. As she sat wondering, Ivana wandered elsewhere with her ceaseless rounds of greetings, a thinly disguised way to keep exercising around the unit. How could the nurses fall for that? They were mostly student nurses today, that's how. The regulars wouldn't allow Ivana such liberties.

Anise flipped quickly through the Oxford Dictionary, searching for the right word to record in her journal:

Institutionalized: 1896. [Late Middle English and French] 1. The dull monotony of institutionalized life. 2. Lacking the will or ability to think and act independently because of having spent a long time in an institution such as a psychiatric hospital or prison.

Also known as 4-Psych-O.

Gawd. I hope I don't turn into Ivana. Please let me keep some sense of independence in this asylum.

Asylum (Middle English). A sanctuary for criminals and debtors, from which they cannot be forcibly taken without violation or escape. Lunatic asylum (1776).

Lunacy: 1541. (Middle English and French). 1. Intermittent insanity formerly attributed to changes of the moon (See also lunar, lunatic, loon.). Now generally any form of insanity. 2. Mad folly.

It certainly is. Mad folly. To be here. On 4-Psych-O.

At least we don't live in filth or sleep in our own piss and poo, like in the 16th century. And I'm not shackled to the wall. Just this...

The apparatus to her right beeped once, then kept up a series of beeping. A plaintive ugly sound. The nurse, a young woman named Rasheema, entered the bedroom. She smiled at the girls, and touched the keyboard to reset the flow. Anise watched her, and followed the tube from her line of vision just beneath her nose snaking up to the trellis that held the Ensure. Strawberry. Anise could taste it when she burped. She'd been tube-fed for close to two weeks, now. She hated the feeling of the tube in her nose, tried to forget it, thought about pulling it out often, had wrenched it in her sleep. Yesterday, she'd begged Dr. Z to remove it. Monday, he'd said. Monday. Two days from now. At least the intravenous was gone from her arm. Potassium. Her body was all out of whack.

> Well, I've known that little secret for years. My body out of whack. You just have to look at the mags and MuchMusic videos to see how out of whack I am. Seems to me like some of those models and actresses should be in here instead of me.
>
> body out of whack
>
> body disgust
>
> > large-boned
> > big-hipped
> > thick ankles
> > fat ass
>
> body desired
>
> > emaciated
> > skeletal
> > thin body
> > thin body
>
> then I'd be somebody somebody instead of nobody nobody

it would be good
  in a way
to have no body

Anise shut her journal, set it on the rolling cart of the machine, and wheeled out of the room. Down the hall she spied Ivana again. The woman was definitely institutionalized, and although she spoke often about leaving, Anise could see no evidence that Ivana would ever leave. Irrepressibly happy, Ivana seldom talked about her disease, but continually cheered the others on in their recovery, all the while refusing to sit down, rest, take meds, eat. Clearly, she was the skinniest woman on the ward. Everyone said so. But while Anise, on the one hand, admired Ivana's willpower, on the other, she saw the yellowness of her skin, her thinning hair, her grayish teeth. And she'd overheard the nurses talking. Ivana was faring worse and worse. Anise believed it.

"Hey, Anise." Here it comes again. Predictable as a skipping cd, "How are you feeling?"

Like shit. "Fine, Ivana." Just as lousy as you are. And just the same as a few minutes ago. The last time you asked. But Anise said none of this. Instead, wheeled past to the eating room where several women and girls were seated at various tables. An art volunteer was working with them. They were making butterflies and angels.

Puke, Anise thought. Just what I need. Cherubs and papillons. She wandered into the tv room and lost herself in the banality of the daytime soaps.

At 4:30 it was time for meds. Dutifully, the anorexics and the bulimics and the binge-purgers and the screw-ups of 4-Psych-O marched towards the tiny room. The one kept tightly locked. There, a smiling nurse made bad jokes and handed small paper cups to each of the inmates.

Anise accepted hers. Nurse Lu watched her take the medication, put it into her mouth. Anise thought about not swallowing. About pocketing the pills in the side of her cheek and pretending. Anise was good at secrets and hiding stuff. This time she chose to swallow. Lu nodded approvingly when Anise opened her mouth and stuck out her tongue as proof.

In half an hour it would be feed time. Anise grimaced, sat down in a corner chair near the end of the ward, wrapped a blanket around her cold self, began to copy from the textbook she'd found in the hospital library:

Any number of psychological disturbances are present in anorexics, including asceticism and a pathological sense of self. Those diagnosed with anorexia nervosa are notoriously hard to treat.

Ascetic: 1646. [Latin or Greek] 1. Of or pertaining to the Ascetics, or to the exercise of rigorous self-discipline; severely abstinent, austere. 2. One of those who in the early church retired into solitude, to exercise themselves in meditation and prayer, and in the practice of rigorous self-discipline by celibacy, fasting, and toil 1673. 3. One who is extremely rigorous in self-denial 1660.

Celibacy: 1663. [Latin] unmarried, bachelor; the state of living unmarried.

Ha ha, OED. I know what celibacy means. No screwing around. For love of god! Well, I haven't screwed around in some time... not counting that humiliating drunken mistake that happened with Marcel's friend, Darcy, on the rec room couch. Shit. That was certainly worth forgetting.

Worth abstinence. Worth celibating. Ha ha.

Pathology: 1611. [French or Latin] 1. The science or study of disease. 2. The sum of morbid processes or conditions 1672, extended to the study of morbid or abnormal mental or moral conditions 1842.

Notorious: 1548. [Latin] 1. Of facts: well known; forming a matter of common knowledge 1555. 2. Famous 1555. 3. Conspicuous; obvious, evident 1770. 4. Noted for some bad practice, quality, etc.; unfavourably known or spoken of 1579.

Soooooo. That means I'm famous. That I'm unfavourably known or spoken of due to my psychological state of near-religious madness driving me to renounce sex in favour of mad dieting further leading me to a preoccupation with death and self-hatred making me conspicuously a hopeless lunatic case.

Loony. Crazy.

That's what I thought, too.

So if the experts and I are in agreement, why do I have to go to the feed lot room?

Anise closed her journal and trudged, slack-slippered, towards the dreaded chamber. And the evening eating ritual began.

Trays were delivered and doled out to the girls and women who sat crowded around the tables with ugly table cloths.

"Dinner is served. Bon appetit!" Rasheema beamed at the patients and took her place at the chair near the door.

Solemnly, they began. Helen in the corner took her spoon and carefully began to squeeze her cottage cheese, removing the milky fluid meticulously from bowl to napkin. Zoe pulled the crusts off her bread and gingerly took a bite from its centre. She chewed and chewed. Ivana spent five minutes shaking several spices all over her food. Lydia began gulping her food until Sue Ann, one of the nurses, put her hand on her shoulder and whispered something in her ear. The room was very quiet. Joyless. Clink of cutlery against plates. Heads bent in misery.

We do look a little like ascetic monks, Anise thought.

One or two other nurses asked the girls about their days. Some of the older outpatients—those who were getting better—spoke softly to one another.

Anise looked glumly at the peas on her plate. She'd formed them into a geometric pattern. Now Rasheema was eyeing her. Anise took her fork and lanced a few peas. Directed her hand to her mouth. Opened it and permitted the peas entry.

At that moment she hated Dr. Z. She hated the loathsome and witless parental units. Hated these other freaks. Hated the nurses. Hated. All of them. And herself. For doing this. To her.

Anise swallowed her peamush. Like a good anorexic. Or bad. Depending on whose point of view.

And Anise felt very bad.

Chapter four

You know you have anorexia when...

- you measure your days by the tape measure around your thighs and butt
- you don't measure up and your measurements are too big
- food intake is the only thing you control
- weak equals eating; strong equals not eating
- you spend half an hour in the grocery store debating the merits of fat free chips vs fat free yogurt and then choose neither
- you congratulate yourself for being hungry, because being hungry means you're a good anorexic
- you obsess over cookbooks and food magazines
- when you're not thinking about weight you're thinking about food
- even when you're not thinking about food, you're thinking about food

GAIL SIDONIE SOBAT

- you dream about food
- you weigh yourself three times before noon
- you weigh yourself three times after noon
- you are the value of the number on that scale
- you never, ever, under any circumstances drink any pop unless it's diet soda
- you thrive on laxatives
- then obsess that they might have calories
- you are absolutely terrified of pizza
- and cheese on anything
- you exercise for three hours because you allowed yourself a 30-calorie snack
- you're continually cold and shivering, even though it's summer
- you're happy your potassium levels are low because that means you're a good little anorexic
- you're happy your period has stopped because that means you're a good little anorexic
- you wish you could be as skinny as that other girl, or that one over there, or better yet, skinnier than either of them
- you know the calorie count of absolutely every food

- you perfect a regime of eating patterns that fool your family and friends into thinking you've just eaten
- you go to the grocery store just to practice not buying the high caloric foods
- the occasional times you do eat are always in front of friends and family so that they'll be tricked into thinking that you're eating normally
- you drink gallons of water
- or you don't drink any because you are terrified of water weight
- you watch food commercials as if they're horror movies
- you cannot eat in front of friends or guys because they'll think you are a fat pig
- if someone tells you that you're looking healthy you exercise three more hours that night because you translate what they say as meaning you're fat
- you know you are the fattest person in the school
- you are embarrassed and disgusted and ashamed of your fat self
- you hate mirrors
- but you find them irresistible
- your hair is falling out

GAIL SIDONIE SOBAT

- you smoke because it burns calories and suppresses appetite
- you drink lots of coffee or take caffeine pills because caffeine suppresses appetite
- you avoid vitamin pills because they might have calories
- you buy diet pills like junkies buy smack
- you spend thousands of dollars in a year on diuretics
- throwing up makes you feel the best you have all day
- sick and starving are "in"
- you always take the stairs
- you load your backpack with as many books as possible because the extra weight helps to burn calories
- you know all the pro-ana/mia sites on the Internet and have them saved under "favourites"
- you know what pro-ana/mia means
- thin equals perfect
- your thinspirations are Kate Moss, Christine Alt, Mary-Kate Olsen, Whitney Houston, Calista Flockhart, Courtney Cox, Nicole Ritchie
- anorexia is your best friend because you don't have any others anymore

GRAVITY JOURNAL

- cutting is the only way you cope, or if that fails, piercing or tattooing or tanning to blackness are your next best options
- you dress in layers to hide your body from well-meaning friends who are concerned, but still you are convinced that you are fat, fat, fat
- you believe and will always believe and will never let go of the fact that you are fat, fat, fat
- you would rather die than be fat, fat, fat

Chapter five

Dr. Z—aka Satan—lied to me. He said I'd get my tube out on Monday. It's been a week and a half since then, and I've still got plastic shoved down into my gut. My nose is rubbed raw, so I have to put Vaseline on it. Great. I look like a creature from a horror flick:

> Frankenstein. Frankanise.
> Alien. Alien Anise. Alienated.
> Freakshow. Freakanise.

Thirty-six hundred. 3600.
I can't believe it. If I want the tube out today, I must agree to consume 3600 calories per day. Per diem.
Puke.
Only wait. Can't do that either. I'm on "close." Which means that every time I need to do pee pee or take a shit, I am watched through the little window of my bedroom bathroom. It means that I wear an ugly orange wristband that denotes not only that I'm crazy, but that I'm so crazy I must be watched closely. It means that I am treated worse than a child, like an infant, because I might puke up my cookies—not that I eat cookies EVER—or take

a diuretic or laxative or horde or hide my food or cut or take my own meaningless life.

    I hate this frickin' wristband. I hate the colour orange.

    At least I'm not like Ivana, now on "constant watch." She's not allowed to stand or walk without permission. They even had to spoonfeed her on the weekend. To preserve her energy. She's that weak. That sick. How come she's not on a tube, I wonder?

    They all hate me here. That's why.

    Ivana, they like. Because she's always so pleasant and nice-y nice-y. Barf. If you're nice or sweet or blonde or pretty on 4-Psych-O, you get treated better. You really do.

    And I'm none of those things.

    And Lu, the night charge nurse, especially hates me. She says I'm manipulative and hurtful. That she sees through my pathetic attempts to get attention. Isn't fooled by my acting out. Knows what I really need. I asked her what that was. She just smirked. Probably thinks I could use a stint in the army. Or maybe overseas working for Oxfam or Unicef where I could see what real suffering is. As if I don't know. As if seeing others suffer is the answer to my problems. That if I see a bunch of skinny starving kids I'll just come to my senses.

    It's amazing how many people think that's all we need here. It's amazing that nurses even think that. It's amazing that they hire those kind of people to be nurses. Those kind of people are anything but kind.

    Well. I fixed Lu, didn't I?

GRAVITY JOURNAL

Last night she was peering in my little window to see what I was doing on the toilet. So I showed her. Yes, I did. I took the piece of toilet paper that I was using to wipe my ass at that very moment, and I showed her just what I was up to. Held it aloft. My shatty asswipe. Towards her ugly face at the window. And the look on that face when I did it... priceless.

She told Dr. Z and he gave me a lecture. "Anise! When are you going to grow up? Start acting your age? Stop manipulating? Bla bla bla, Anise."

Yeah, well. Maybe I'm not interested in acting my age. Becoming an adult. Maybe I look around at this world and the idiot adults in it, and I've decided I want no part of all that. Maybe I just hate the idea of succumbing to the suburban dreams of my parents and their martini-swilling friends. Maybe I hate you, Dr. Z and all that you stand for. Why would I want to be like you with your stale breath and your hopeless comb-over and your shell of a life? Maybe I can see the writing on the hospital wall. And I don't like what I read between the lines, so why should I just go there? To that adult place? Let me stay here. Or let me end it before I get there. Seem like two good options to me.

Anyways, I apologized to Lu. And I've agreed to the thirty-six hundred gross calories. So I'll play their stupid game and get fat, fat, fat. And ugly. More ugly than I already am.

Ugly Anise ugly Anise ugly Anise ugly.

Chapter Six

Anise sat in the small hospital schoolroom brightly decorated with the trappings of elementary classrooms. The alphabet in colourful animal letters across one wall. Pictures of the planets floating above the teacher's desk. Stuffed animals and beanie babies flopping here and there on chairs and the computer stations. All very gay.

Mornings the school served as the classroom for other sick kids in Eliza Petraclark Memorial. Afternoons, however, were devoted entirely to the skeletal students of 4-Psych-O. Herself included. The fattest girl on the ward. Well to her mind, anyway.

Anise and three other unit girls sat silent at four identical desks. Waiting for the teachers who were in the next room photocopying. Amanda had her Social Studies text and binder neatly before her. Zoe had her Biology open and was biting her fingernails, scanning the material she felt sure she didn't know. Her head buried in her arms across her desk, Erica looked ill-prepared for math. Anise's books were still in her backpack. She couldn't be bothered to unzip and fish out her English notebook. Instead, she listened to Cat Power on her iPod and stared glumly at the cheery surroundings.

The teachers, Ms. Dobbin and Mr. Rowe, re-entered the room. Bringing along their incessantly sunny smiles. Which irked Anise. Who grew further irked when smiley Ms. Dobbin insisted she remove her headphones, put away the iPod, and get out her notebook. Anise complied, sighing.

Mr. Rowe turned to the other girls and distributed the personal info sheets, still warm from the photocopier. He seemed to have a great deal of difficulty handing out two sheets of paper to each and managed to give himself a paper cut in the process. Anise noticed that a button was missing from his shirt and the sleeves were too short for his lanky arms. Mr. Rowe drew a hand through his mop of hair and chuckled at himself. He sat in a tiny child-sized chair near to Zoe and coached her in completing her form.

As Anise filled out her info sheet, she secretly studied the woman teacher. Who looked to be anywhere between twenty-eight to forty-five. Whatever. Old. And dressed well... her clothes weren't ugly. But different. Everything matched. Shoes. Handbag. Outfit or whatever you wanted to call it. All perfectly plum coloured. Even the brooch, a little mermaid swimming with a pearl in her hand, and matching pearl earrings. The skirt was ankle length and the top a little low cut. For a teacher. Anyways.

And they were both so enthusiastic. Maddeningly so. The girls just couldn't or wouldn't rise to their optimism. But that didn't seem to daunt Ms. Dobbin or Mr. Rowe, oh no. She was thrilled with each of their names. He was excited to learn which schools they attended. Both were tickled to hear what their personal goals were for their stay at the school. Geez. Did they never stop smiling?

And moving around the room? It made Anise dizzy. One moment Dobbin was helping Amanda with the French Revolution. Another she was looking something up in a reference text to help Zoe, who wasn't even her student—she was actually working with Mr. Rowe, who, they learned, was the science and math teacher. But that didn't stop Mr. Rowe from voicing his opinions on anything to do with literature or history. He wandered over to see what Anise thought of the star-cross'd lovers and then Ms. Dobbin flitted by to find out where exactly Anise was in her Romeo and Juliet unit. The woman seemed to know a great deal about Shakespeare. She could recite the whole "But soft, what light through yonder window" speech. That was cool at least. About the Shakespeare. Which Anise loved. And Rowe seemed to know a lot about science and a little about absolutely everything else.

Anise turned her attention back to the info sheet.

Name: *Anise Jasmine Luther*

Age: *16*

Address: *3958 Riverbend Road, Edmonton, AB Canada*

Last School Attended: *King Edward Academy of the Arts*

Grade: *10 or 11, depending*

Home Phone Number: *780 444 7685*

Parents' Work Number: *780 885 7485*

Parents' names: *Loathed and Witless*

Subjects you are taking this term: *English 10, Math 20, Science 10, French 20*

Objectives while in the hospital school: *To maintain my honours average and stay caught up with my work.*

Personal interests and hobbies:

Anise thought for a moment. Should she tell this man and this woman that cutting was her favourite pastime? Suicide plots? Ha. That'd wipe the smiles off the teachers' faces, wouldn't it? She thought about it. Telling the truth. Thought about substituting her parents' names, "Loathed and Witless," for their real names, "Deirdre and Trent." Decided to go with the lies on the hobbies and Anise's personal truth about their names. See what these teachers would do.

Personal interests and hobbies:

I like music. All kinds. But especially alternative stuff like the Smith's and Franz Ferdinand. I don't much like mainstream. Ok, maybe just a few bands. I like art. Drawing. Painting. Putting stuff together from trash. And I like Shakespeare. Well, English, in general. So please don't ruin it for me by making me dissect every little thing with reference and allusion. Ok. That's about it. My life is boring.

Ms. Dobbin took her sheet, glanced once at it and nodded, handed it to Mr. Rowe who read it, nodded, then set it with the others. Dobbin asked Anise to keep reading Act III of the play where she'd left off. Although tired from her meds, Anise managed to read most of it.

Two hours flew by. It wasn't as boring as being on the ward. A kind of change, actually. At 3 pm, Ms. Dobbin walked the four girls back to 4-Psych-O because they were all on "close" and needed supervision to and from the ward. They said good-bye to the smiling woman. And Anise actually found herself looking forward to tomorrow's class.

Mr. Rowe and Ms. Dobbin were really quite a pair. The classroom was the oddest classroom Anise had ever attended. And she'd been to a number of schools. Kicked out of two already. Before she'd been admitted to the hospital, she'd attended the King Edward Academy of the Arts, which despite its royal name was actually a good school for kids who were into drama or music or dance or film or visual or performing arts. Which Anise was. So she was kind of glad that she'd got sick before getting kicked out of this last one. Her parents had fought hard to get her in to King Edward Academy. Well, it suited them, didn't it? At least they could brag about something. A prestigious school for their irritating, sick daughter. At least they had that.

But Mr. Rowe and Ms. Dobbin weren't anything like other teachers, even the arts teachers Anise had known. For one thing, they let the students swear. A lot. Without blinking an eye. Another thing is that they never sat in desks. They sat with the students and worked individually with them. And another thing. They were very loud.

"Are ye sure that's the correct answer to the math question then, laddie?" smiling Ms. Dobbin shouted in mock Scots accent across the small room.

"Aye, 'tis Woman! Do ye think I'm daft then?" Mr. Rowe raised a bushy eyebrow in pretend outrage.

"Sure! Ye're a daft bugger, Mr. Rowe. I've said it afore, and I'll say it agin!"

And the two would burst into cackles as though truly delighted with themselves. And then ten minutes later:

"Ve have vays of instructing you in za the finer points of physics. Und ve vill insist zat zese students verk verry verry hard und become like Albert Einstein, ya Fraulein Dobbin?"

"Yavolt, Herr Rowe. Indeed, ve have our vays!" And they would affect Nazi-teacher poses in a silly attempt to make the students laugh, because by now everyone knew what relaxed and agreeable teachers they were.

Throughout the afternoon, as Ms. Dobbin marched her students across Europe in history, she'd take on a different accent for each region, and Mr. Rowe, though working on biology, would chime in with the corresponding accent. And they'd crack each other up. It was dumb. But funny, too, in a stupid way. They weren't afraid to be clowns.

When a student completed an essay, Rowe and Dobbin would enact a little essay dance in celebration.

When a student had a particularly good mark on an assignment, Rowe and Dobbin would make a huge (and loud) announcement. Give the student (a high school student!) any number of kiddie stickers.

When a student was tired, they'd make a pot of coffee.

When a student was sad, they'd give her a stuffed teddy bear as a small consolation gift.

When students whined or complained or ranted, they'd listen. Attentively.

When a student smiled or laughed at a joke, Rowe and Dobbin practically crapped themselves with joy.

When the students arrived, Rowe and Dobbin were genuinely glad to see them.

Anise liked coming to class.

• • • • •

"These are lobelia plants," Ms. Dobbin beamed across a tray of bright blue miniature blooms. "I'm rather partial to them myself. And I brought one for each of you." She set the bedding tray down on the large table that she'd covered with newspaper. "First though, we'll have to paint these clay pots." Ms. Dobbin gave each of the five girls a pot and set out an egg container filled with vivid acrylic paints.

"I thought this was supposed to be Social Studies class for me," Amanda whined.

"And Bio for me," Zoe added.

"Vell, ve can all use a little diversion every once in a while, eh Fraulein Dobbin?" Mr. Rowe's basso-profundo voice rumbled. He'd entered the room, his usual rumpled clothes covered by a green artist's apron. He distributed aprons to the girls and took a chair at the table beside them. A grinning Ms. Dobbin handed him a clay pot and set a jar of paintbrushes in the centre of the table.

"Vell, go to it you little artistes!"

At Mr. Rowe's encouragement, Anise shrugged. Donned an apron and took up the final terracotta pot.

She selected dark purple for the base coat of her pot, since there was no black to be had. Anise actually liked the rich purple colour. Aubergine. That was what it was called. Anise knew that aubergine was fancy-ass for eggplant. Still it sounded good. Exotic.

She turned to Ms. Dobbin. "Do you have any artbooks in this school?"

"You mean the kind with colour prints of the masters? We sure do!" And she practically tripped over herself to get to the bookshelf in the corner. "What are you interested in?"

"Van Gogh."

"I have a whole book on just Van Gogh!" She pronounced it "Goch" like a fishbone was caught in her throat. Handed the text triumphantly to Anise.

"Thanks." Anise opened the book, seeking the painting she liked best. Not "Starry Night," although that was a good painting. She preferred "Crows over the Wheatfield." Van Gogh's last painting.

Anise's acrylic coat was nearly dry. Patiently, she began to paint the wheat field at the base of the small pot. Golds and yellows and russets in similar broad strokes to those of the master. Her tongue in the corner of her mouth, Anise traced the violent swaying of the wheat, the undulating path cutting a swath through the middle. She paused to observe the Van Gogh and to allow the paint to dry. Anise glanced around the table.

The others were finished decorating their pots. One had painted daisies all around. Melody had designed musical notes and written her name in a florid script. Another pot was simply a solid crimson. Mr. Rowe's pot was kind of an ugly disaster, but he was smiling like an imbecile, delighted with his project.

Anise took up another paintbrush, swirled it around in the indigo paint, swirled it onto her pot, counterwise to the direction of the wheat. It made her angry. They just rushed through. And she was only half done.

Ms. Dobbin was demonstrating how to transplant the small bedding plants into the larger pots, those that were completely dry. Potting soil spilled over onto the newspaper and splotches of paint were everywhere.

"Take your time, Anise. There's no hurry." To the others, she opined,

"I'd like you to take care of these plants. They're symbols, you know."

What teacher could resist the opportunity for a lecture? Anise didn't look at Ms. Dobbin, but felt the woman's eyes on her.

Dobbin: "I think of them as all of you. Tender young green shoots that need love and attention."

Rowe: "And only you can give it to them."

Dobbin: "Right. So when you water these little blooms, think of the idea of watering yourself. Tending to your own blossoms. Your own blossoming. Take care of you."

Rowe: "Because in the final analysis. You're the only ones who can."

Ordinarily, it would have seemed corny. Should have. But Dobbin's and Rowe's voices were kind. Sincere. Their words were comforting.

Mr. Rowe leaned over Anise's shoulder. "Don't worry about having to finish on time." It was three minutes to three. "We've got work to do after school, so you can go on painting, Anise."

She said nothing in reply, but secretly, Anise was relieved. She absorbed herself into the pattern of the flying crows she was creating.

At 4:07, the schoolroom was quiet, but for the occasional whirring of the photocopy machine. Anise was finished and the paint was dry. She admired her work. It was a respectable reproduction.

Ms. Dobbin looked in on her from the other room. "That's a very fine piece," she said softly. "So much going on, in the original... and in yours. So much movement. Such an artist must have an active — and troubled imagination."

Anise nodded. Knew which artist Dobbin referred to. Not the dead guy. But Anise. No one had ever called her an artist before.

She allowed Ms. Dobbin to help her with the planting.

"How old are you?"

Her teacher smiled, "As old as my tongue and a little older than my teeth."

Anise smiled. "I've heard that before somewhere."

"Probably at Christmastime. It's from the book, *Miracle on 34th Street*. But it's true, nonetheless."

Ms. Dobbin walked Anise back to the ward. The small plant balanced brightly atop her books.

That night Anise wrote:

Ageless. Like a Van Gogh painting. Ms. Dobbin.

chapter Seven

Anise listened to the words Barlow sang in her headphones:

> *Doesn't matter that you're lying in the gutter,*
> *Doesn't matter that your brains all cluttered,*
> *Doesn't matter that you're covered in scars,*
> *You're never in the gutter with your eyes on the stars.*
> *Walk away.*

She loved the song. But if it were only that easy. To walk away from anorexia. Back off from bulimia. Keep my eyes on the stars.

Each day a struggle.
Tomorrow and tomorrow and tomorrow.

She understood Shakespeare's repetition. Profoundly. Yesterday was hard. So was today. So would be tomorrow. And tomorrow.

Anise glanced at her night table. Her toothbrush and Sensodyne toothpaste. Now she had to use old-people toothpaste. The hospital dentist who was re-constructing her teeth had told her. Too much puking had worn away the enamel of her teeth.

Shit.

Anise picked up her hand mirror and grimaced at herself. Still he was doing a nice job of it. The handsome intern dentist. Not her type. But not bad for eye candy.

Ha! The only candy she'd allow herself. Other than the sugar-free candy Mr. Rowe and Ms. Dobbin kept in a jar in the classroom.

Although today I did also enjoy the frozen yogurt. Mango. Delicious. Even if it hurt my old lady teeth.

Anise took her water glass and padded past Zoe's sleeping form. She spilled the contents into her lobelia plant, now bursting with blue blossoms. She loved the little plant. Fussed over it. Beamed when Fran, her favourite nurse, admired her painted pot.

Satisfied the plant was doing well, she returned to her bed. Checked the time. 3 am. Still not sleepy. These new meds were playing havoc with her body clock. She'd have to tell Dr. Z tomorrow. Try to convince him she knew best. Not bloody likely.

Today, Rose the gossipy nurse told me about Amber, a girl who used to be on 4-Psych-O. A girl who ate things. Not food. She hated food. But liked to eat things. Knives. Forks. Pencils. Erasers. Sticks.

She even ate her bedclothes.

Okay. That's freaky. I may be sick. But not that sick.

I guess she died. They operated on her too many times. Or she took her life. From misery.

Kind of like the Elephant Man. John Merrick. I read the play and watched the movie this week with Ms. Dobbin. John was physically very sick and disfigured. Beyond belief, really. A kind of monster. The make-up they did on that actor was very convincing. Just like the medical photographs of the real Elephant Man. Anyways, he wanted to be normal. Like everyone else. Like we all do. Like I do. But he couldn't ever be. Not with such a horrible condition.

But he had friends and moments of happiness. And then the freak killed himself. That made me mad. I wanted him to live. To go on. I guess he couldn't. Like Amber couldn't. Too much pain.

John Merrick, the most compassionate person in the play and the movie, wanted to sleep normally, lying down. He knew it would kill him. Crush his windpipe from the weight of his disfigured head. But he wanted to sleep. Perchance to dream. Like I do now. Except. That I can't. My mind is too full.

Do I want to die?

Do I?

Anise looked at herself in the hand mirror again. She looked for one good thing to like about herself, just as Ms. Dobbin had instructed her to do. Ms. Dobbin, who had so much to like about herself, tried to convince her students to look for one thing a day to voice out loud that they liked about themselves. It was hard. But Anise peered into the mirror and really tried.

Her skin was so pale it was translucent. Her eyes were shaded in the semi-darkness of the hospital room. Dark circles were half-moons beneath her eyes. A silver ring glinted at her left eyebrow. Her eyebrows were dark and, well there was no other word for it really... shapely. Anise liked her eyebrows. Permitted herself to like her eyebrows. There. That was it then. The one thing today.

Do I? Want to die?

Not today, I guess. I've got these eyebrows. And a cool eyebrow ring from Marcel.

●●●●●

The tiny cellphone vibrated against her leg.

"Hello," her voice a hoarse whisper.

"Hey, Licorice Breath! It's me."

"Marcel. You're drunk!"

"You got it, little sister! Pissed to the bejesus!"

"It's Wednesday night, for gawd sake, Mars."

"Thurzday morning, to be accurate, 'Nise."

"What the hell, Marcel?"

"Hey Allsorts! You're a poet! And don't I know it!"

"Don't you have school tomorrow?"

"Fuck school!" And Marcel's voice was suddenly hard.

"What?"

"You heard me. I'm not going back there. Fuck it."

"Mom and Dad..."

"Fuck them, too. I got kicked out."

"Of school? Of the house? Marcel?" She could hear him taking a swig from some bottle of something.

"Of both, Nise."

"Shit Mars."

"Sure is. But the shittiest... Alana broke up with me."

"That bitch!"

"She was the best..." Marcel's voice began to crumble, "the best thing in my life, Anise."

"Oh Marcel." What could she say? Anise had never liked Alana. Good riddance she was gone. But that wasn't what he wanted or needed to hear. She searched for the right words. "Hey, Mars. It'll be ok. You can get through this."

Marcel did not or could not speak. She heard his breathing, ragged and sob-ridden. She tried again.

"Marcel, you still have me. I'm here for you." She almost puked at that one. How much help could she be to him while incarcerated in

4-Psych-O? Shit, she hated this. Her brother needed her and here she was letting him down. "Look, come by tomorrow, ok? We can hang together and talk this through. Just stop drinking, ok, Mars?"

Anise knew what he was drinking and how it would be. Jack Daniels. A mickey, at least. Marcel would drink himself stupid or sick or poisoned or all three.

"Ok, Marcel?"

She could hear him wiping his snotty nose on his sleeve. "Yeah."

"Pour the rest out, right now!"

"There's only a little left."

"I don't care. Take this phone with you to the can and I want to hear you pouring." Anise's voice was firm. Parental.

"Shit, Anise."

"Do it!"

She heard him walking. A light flicking on. Liquid splashing. A glass bottle dropped presumably into a trash can.

"Fine. I'm done." Marcel's words slurred unhappily.

"Listen, where are you?"

"In the can."

"Mars, I mean whose place are you at?"

"Kevn's."

"Where is he?"

"Passed out already. Crashed."

"So you've got a place to stay."

"Yeah."

"Marcel. Are you on anything else?"

"Naw. Just the JD."

"Ok. Go to sleep, will you? Sleep this off. Tomorrow we'll talk. I'll get a pass and we can go somewhere here at the hospital for coffee. Ok? Mars, promise me you'll be here and that you're alright."

"Fine. All right. Promise."
"Marcel, I'm here, ok? I...love you."
"Thanks, 'Nise." He sounded sleepy.
"Good night, Mars."

She turned off her cellphone and slumped back in bed. How would she sleep now? Her brother. Such a screw-up. She needed to get out of this place to help him. That meant no messing up. No cutting. No purging. No funny food business like hiding or hoarding. Take the full 3600 calories. So that she could take care of Marcel. Who always turned to her in need. After he got busted and had to do community hours. Whenever the parental units pissed him off or fought with him. When he was confused or hurting. Doing too many drugs. Self-destructing. Marcel turned to Anise.

She turned back to her journal.

Do I? Want to die?
Not today, I guess. I've got these eyebrows.
And Marcel needs me.

Chapter eight

Marcel looked like roadkill.

"Drink some more water." Anise pushed the paper cup towards her brother. Then she ripped open six Sweet and Lo packets and poured them in her coffee. "Have you got a place to stay for a while?"

"Yeah. Kevn's."

"Ok. So that's a start. What about work?"

"Still got my job at Canadian Tire."

"Good." She looked abstractedly at the scars along her arms, her white hospital bracelet. "So you screwed up a term at school. So you'll go back."

"I guess."

"No! You don't guess, Marcel. You will! And later... in a few weeks or so you can think about if you want to go home."

"Yeah. If."

"Well, one day I'll be there again. And I could sure use the company, Mars."

"When do you think?"

"Well, it's only been a week since I got off 'close.' I've got a long way to go to reach my goal weight. But someday."

Marcel nodded, but Anise wasn't convinced he was really paying attention. Why should he? This was her third hospitalization for anorexia. She felt her shoulders droop. She'd needed the milestone of getting off close observation. Of losing that stupid orange bracelet to be a celebration. To mark the occasion with someone. She'd hoped that someone would be Marcel.

But it wasn't.

He was in no shape. Lousy shape actually. That meant putting her own stuff—good or bad—on hold to help him.

It made her angry. She swallowed.

Anise could see she wasn't making much headway with this wayward brother of hers. Taking a deep breath, she broached the subject she dreaded.

"Have you heard from her? Alana?"

"No." And in that negative, she heard the depth of his loneliness. Marcel, who despite his outward bravado and show-off attitude had loved that puke of a girlfriend. For some reason. And no matter how stupid Anise thought Alana, she had to say the right thing to her heartsore big brother. She herself had so little to offer about affairs of the heart. Except what she'd read in books. She could only think of the inane.

"I'm sorry, Marcel." Anise tried again. "Look, I don't know exactly what you're feeling. I only know what Hollywood shows me. Or what I've read in novels. But I think the experts say much the same thing. You need time. Probably lots of time. But... it will be better... you'll be better. Again."

Marcel began to tear up. He shook his head morosely. "I doubt it, 'Nise."

"I don't, Mars. You've got all you need to heal and get over her. Besides she doesn't deserve you. Never did."

Marcel looked, really looked, at his sister. "Strange words."

"What?"

"Yours. 'Got all I need to heal.' Strange words. Coming from you. An anorexic."

Anise didn't know whether to cry or slap him.

Who am I?

Anorexic.
Anise. Anise the anorexic.
Nice work, Marcel. Dumbass. Kick a girl when she's down. Label me just like the others have. I expected better from you, mon frére.
And just because I'm ill doesn't mean I can't try to help you. Does it?
Or maybe nothing I say matters because...Anise is an anorexic.
Well, guess what?
I am not an anorexic. I am not my disease.

Who am I?

I awoke this morning with a stranger in my bed. I don't remember going to sleep with this someone, but this morning, when the nurse came in to rouse us, there she was.
Only this. The nurse didn't see her. Neither did Zoe, my roommate. Just me. I gave my head a shake. Still there. Squinched my eyes. Didn't work. She still sat upright beside me, taking up too much room of my already cramped hospital bed.
I looked at her. She at me. What was going on? I pinched her. She pinched back.
"Ouch!"
"Humm?" Zoe murmured from beneath her covers on the other side of the room.
"Who are you?" I hissed at my unwelcome interloper.
"No. Who are YOU?" my bedmate hissed back.
"I? I am a nutbar!"

But she shook her head. And then, of course, I recognized her. I saw the green pajama bottoms and the striped tank top. The tummy slightly protruding. Remnants of a fake tattoo of a Celtic cross on her shoulder. A long neck framed by dark hair. Pointed chin. Sharp nose. Two fine eyebrows arched cleverly. My eyebrow ring.

"Nice eyebrows." I told her.

She just smiled.

Who am I?

"Anise" is an ancient, ancient herb. A flavouring. It was used to avert the evil eye. To stir up lust. Keep away nightmares, if placed under the pillow. Anise oil was used in soaps, perfumes, medicines. Liqueurs and liquours. Like Anisette, Pernot, Ouzo, Raki. Or deadly absinthe which destroyed minds.

Anise sweetened the breath of pharaohs. Made caesars fart to relieve their flatulence. Soothed coughs and throats. Was an effective bait for mice and rats. But poisonous to pigeons. Flavoured candies, pastries, soups, wedding cakes. Cured everything, it seems, from hiccups to epilepsy to nausea to toothache to bronchitis to headache.

Mr. Rowe found a recipe for anise tea on the web, and Ms. Dobbin bought some dried anise leaves at the health food store. We had a regular little tea party. A celebration of my being off 'close.'

They noticed, at least.

I didn't mind the taste. Like I expected... a little like licorice. Which is a diuretic. But we only had a cup each. With Dr. Z's permission. So I think we'll all live. Besides, I promised them all to avert any evil (like diarrhea) so we're safe.

Mr. Rowe launched into a scatological story about how he once crapped his pants in a theatre and had to abandon his ginch in the bathroom stall. I can only imagine the shock of the next visitor to the can.

It was a good enough afternoon.

I hardly thought of what Marcel said to me.

Kind of like that my name is ancient. And that Anise has the power to do harm. Or good.

Who am I?

●●●●●

Once at a different sort of tea party...

She sits reading, pristine in her black cocktail dress with grandmother's pearls at her neck. Above her the antique clock ticks away in boredom. Over the timepiece, my grandmother presides, frozen-faced, brow furrowed by slight surprise as if caught by a camera flash rather than the master's paintbrush. When my mother finally looks up at me, over the open page of her magazine —some artsy woman's glossy—when Mother looks at me with her china blue eyes, so does my grandmother and her mother before her. I keep my brown eyes on my mother and do not let her in.

"You're home early."

"Actually. I'm late."

She glances at the clock. "Right. Time slipped away this afternoon." She reaches for her teacup. Poises the saucer on her lap then raises the cup to her lips. It is Earl Grey. It always is. That's all she drinks. Except for martinis and expensive red wine and scotch.

She grasps the afghan cover and throws it over her shoulders. It wouldn't suit to turn up the heat. Not on a chilly February afternoon. My mother loves to brace for life. Well, she must brace for what is coming this week.

"You'll be getting a call from the doctor."

"Pardon me?"

"I fainted in class." I shrug. "Miss Short drove me to the clinic."

"Which class?"

"Phys Ed."

"But you're in such fine shape. All that exercising."

"Yeah. Well. She'll be calling. She wants to run tests."

"It's probably just some female thing. You know how your time of month affects you sometimes."

I don't point out that I've stopped having my time of month.

"Anyway. That's what happened."

"Really. Are you feeling terribly poorly?"

"Not so terribly now, thanks."

"Because I could ask cook to whip you up something special."

"No thanks, Mother. I ate on the way home."

She raises an eyebrow, and I hasten to avert suspicion in my practiced way. "Miss Short drove me home and we stopped for a wrap. Her treat."

"Oh. I'll have to drop her a little note."

"You do that, Mother."

She shakes her head at my sarcasm. "Honestly, Anise. I don't know who you are anymore."

When did you ever? Know me? Or really want to? I swallow all that and turn away.

She has already returned to her book.

Who am I?

chapter Nine

under the fashion doll's spell
she taught us
how to walk and talk accessorize
fill our closets with dreams and trifles
have possessions be possessed
if not in full possession of our
selves

we created movies in our minds
daring escapes kidnappings
sometimes we were even heroines
but that's not what she had in mind

showed us the proper attire
for weddings performances
glamour heterosexuality
dates with ken
whoever wherever he is

we so worshipped the Malibu tan
seamless skin

*legs sans cellulite
that we swallowed the whole lie
and little else
now with the dolls
headless or head-shaven
broken or lost or closeted
what do we do with our plastic
selves?*

•••••

"Whatcha writin'?" A lanky form flopped on the couch next to her. Anise sat in the lounge that conjoined the spokes of the various psychiatric wards. She thought she'd have some peace there from the crazies. Nope.

"Poetry." She tried to make her voice sound chilly.

"Really?"

Oh no. That peaked his interest. Anise glanced over her notebook at him. A guy she'd seen before. Many times on this ward.

"Can you read me something?"

"I- uh. It's kind of private."

"Well. Who am I going to tell?"

"I-uh mean. It's personal."

"Can't cha just give me a little hint?"

Geez. This guy was persistent. And slightly annoying. But his interest was also flattering. Anise wondered how her hair looked. Wished she could drop a few pounds like right now. "It's a critique of the fashion doll industry."

"That why you're on this ward? You anorexic?"

"I have anorexia, yes."

"Isn't that a bit simplistic? To blame it all on fashion dolls?"

Hell, this guy had a brain. Anise closed her book, the pen still between the pages as bookmark. "I'm not blaming my disease on fashion dolls."

"No?"

"No. I'm merely saying they're part of a larger, complex problem."

"I'd say so. Every chick I've ever known hates her body. And they're not all locked up here, are they? So somethin's up with that. Me, I don't even like skinny chicks. Oops." He chuckled at his gaffe. "Present company excluded."

Anise coloured. He liked her? When had he even noticed her before? "I'm not skinny."

He regarded her. It was unnerving to have his eyes—one blue, one green—on her. "Whatever. So read me the poem, then."

"You have two different coloured eyes."

"Yup. Hereditary. Like my bi-polar disorder. Read."

So Anise read, blushing the whole way through.

"Hey, what's your name?"

"Anise."

"Anise. Nice. Or Nice. If you're from France." He laughed at his own lame joke. "Well Anise, my name's Boyd, and I'd..."

He was interrupted by the sudden arrival of the musician on the wards. This was a program the hospital sponsored. Every Wednesday, one of the musicians would come to 4-Psych to sing and play for the inmates. Usually some folkie, like this guy, Andy, who was now introducing himself and tuning up his guitar. He began to play.

"Hey, Dylan! Great man!" Anise sat wide-eyed, as Boyd first sang along then rose to dance along to the folksong.

"Hey, Mr. Tambourine man... la la I don't know the words..."

She peered around the room as the loonies from 4-Psych—none of them eating disorder patients—came pouring from their rooms down the various halls of the ward. No one seemed ill at ease with Boyd's dancing. But she was. It was all... so much spectacle.

"I'd better get back." She picked herself up from the sofa and quietly excused herself.

"Hey, Anise! Want to go on a date sometime?" His voice yelled above the music.

Red-faced, she turned back to face the still-dancing Boyd. "A date?"

"Yeah. Somewhere in the hospital, since we're both stuck here. Maybe Friday?"

How to get away from the stares of all the psych patients who'd overheard this subtle invitation and were keenly interested in her response?

"Yeah. Sure. Whatever." Anise bolted from the waiting room.

The psych patients applauded. She wasn't sure if it was for Andy, for Boyd's dancing, or for her affirmative answer.

How utterly embarrassing. But something in her heart made the tiniest flutter.

Butterfly Effect
into this chaos
comes a boy with two-toned eyes
do his wings mark change?

Anise took a bite out of her taco salad, watching Boyd the whole time with her sharp tongue in check. Barely. They sat together in the hospital atrium cafeteria, weak winter light upon their heads.

He was an odd boy, this one. Kinda cute in the right light. But so weird, too. The way his grin came up suddenly, all crooked at the side. And his hair. His hair was a wreck. Not to mention his hospital clothes.

"If we're going to continue this relationship," she half-joked as she watched him gorging on his taco, "the clothes need some serious revisions."

"Huh? My clothes?" Boyd put his taco down and stopped to consider. "I never give clothes much thought."

"Ya huh!"

"I've been in hospital scrubs for too long, I guess."

"I guess."

"Are we in a relationship already?" There was his quirky grin again. "I haven't even kissed you yet!"

Anise wondered why her stomach was flip-flopping.

"But since you're such a good poet, I guess I'd like to continue this 'relationship,' so I'll take you up on your sartorial advice."

Wow. Boyd knew the word "sartorial," even if he didn't have any fashion sense. He was smart. Anise found out that he was in first year of university in comparative literature. Cool.

"Do you know my loathsome parent would kill me if she knew I was out with you?"

"Why? Because I'm crazy? Or just older?"

"Both."

They laughed.

"That's a nice sound Anise. I hardly ever see you smile, let alone laugh."

"When do you see me?"

"I've been watching you for weeks. As I was crawling out from under my rock of depression."

"Stalking."

"Yeah. Right up to the locked glass door of your unit. No. Just watching. I think you're interesting with your Collected Works of Shakespeare and your sketchpad or journal tucked under your arm. Your serious pretty face as you motor down the hall or off the unit."

Anise looked down at her salad. "I noticed you, too."

She thought his face would crack with grinning. "Really? Cool. Then I guess we were destined to meet."

She shrugged. How unnerving this conversation. His presence. "How come you're depressed?"

"I wasn't taking my meds very religiously. In fact, I'd stopped." He sighed. "I guess I know better. But sometimes I feel under water with the lithium. And I'd rather not."

"I know how you feel about meds. I'd like to stop entirely."

"Don't, Anise." He sought out her eyes.

She half-smiled back at him. "Well, I won't stop, if you won't."

"Not gonna. Already messed up half a term at university."

Anise thought about her own missed time at school, but at least she had the hospital school with the comedy team of Dobbin and Rowe. University students in the hospital didn't have that luxury.

"Hey..." he interrupted her thoughts. "It's not all bad. After all, we got to meet, didn't we? That's getting lemonade from your lemons, ain't it?"

Nodding, she took a sip of water. Tried to drive away thoughts about the number of calories in a taco salad.

Boyd went back to devouring his food. Anise envied him that. Devouring. What was it like to devour food? To devour life? She picked at her salad. Looked over at him again. A look of pure rapt pleasure as he ate. Wow. That was cool. Sexy even.

That was it!

This nutcase down the hall from her and her own nutcase ward was sexy. Weird, yes. But sexy. And his attention, his admiration of her, made her feel that way, too. And how long had it been since she'd felt sexy?

"Are you gonna finish that, Anise?"

She looked into his different-coloured eyes. "Yes. I think I am."

Chapter ten

"C'mon, Anise!"

Boyd pulled her up the small staircase to the door. They'd already climbed six flights.

"Aren't you loving this? You told me you took the stairs all the time to burn calories, so I thought this would be your ideal date." He waited at the top for her ascent, fumbled with some sort of lockpick thing, then opened the door to reveal the roof of the Eliza Petraclark Memorial Hospital.

They stepped out to a vista of the entire city agleam in full midday sunlight.

"I don't think we're allowed up here, Boyd."

"And why should that stop us?"

"How did you pick that lock?"

"Guess I neglected to tell you about my summer jobs..."

"B & E?"

"Naw. My dad's a locksmith. I help him out every summer, that is, if I'm doing well enough. He's taught me the tricks of his trade and gave me a set of my own tools for high school graduation."

"Hmmm. Sounds like an invitation to a life of crime to me." She eyed his two-coloured eyes shrewdly.

"Hey! It's an honourable profession that stems back centuries. There'd be many a princess still locked in a lonely tower, if it weren't for locksmiths."

"Not to mention chastity belts still chastely locked against intruders..."

"Hey, do you have one of those? Because if so, I could help you with that-"

"Never mind!" she laughed nervously. Anise walked gingerly towards the edge of the hospital roof and peered over. "I'm not a fan of heights."

"No? They don't bother me."

"Isn't it a little foolhardy for a manic-depressive to have access to a roof?"

"Bi-polar, please. And yes. I've considered coming up here on my darkest days." Boyd stood near her, gazing at the skyline and the river snaking in the valley between the city centre and the hospital. She turned to look at him. The breeze played with her hair.

"That frightens me, Boyd."

"It's ok. I'm ok. Better. These days aren't dark. And soon I'll be getting out of here."

"And you're going to stay on the meds, right?"

"Yep. That's my plan and I'm sticking to it. Anise," he pulled a strand of her dark hair away from her eyes. "When I do leave, I'd like this to continue..."

"What?" she breathed.

"This." And very gently, he kissed her lips.

•••••

Later that afternoon they sat together in the hospital atrium.

sun floods this green place
blossoms on the climbing vines open
like lovers to the light

Boyd leaned on his arm watching her at work in her journal. Occasionally, he took a sip from his coffee, but otherwise kept his eyes fixed. It was unnerving.

"Do you mind?"

"Nope."

"I mean, would you mind not staring?"

"Can't help myself. An artist is before me. Composing a great work of staggering genius."

"I read that book."

"Of course you did. You wrote it."

"Boyd."

"Can I help it if I admire you?"

Wow. This guy who kissed like a movie star. This guy with the good looking grin. Admired her. Anise felt again that now-familiar flutter. And a blush creep into her cheeks.

"Are you finished yet?"

"Finished?"

"Your poem about me."

"I'm not writing about you, Mr. Egotistical."

"Yes. Yes, you are."

"No, I'm not."

"Be that way. All selfish and everything, then." His tone was mock-serious.

"Is this our first argument?"

"Well, that's what I'd do. Write about you, I mean. If I were a writer. Which I'm not. But I'd do it for you. So I think, given your gawd-given talents, that's what you should be doing. For me."

"You're nuts, you know that?"

"Yeah," Boyd leaned in close, "about you." And kissed her again in the atrium sunlight.

•••••

He held her hand as they walked back to the unit. They were about to pass the interfaith chapel when Boyd pulled her inside. The air was cool and hushed. Late afternoon sunlight peered through the stained glass windows. No one was in the room. They peeked behind the screens at the colourful prayer rugs on the floor. Admired the Star of David on the opposite wall. Sniffed at the sweetgrass that awaited lighting in the censor. Rang the Buddhist bell on the small silk-draped table.

"You see. All faiths are welcome. Everyone. Even we crazies." Boyd led her to a pew that faced a modest cross. He closed his eyes and put his hands together briefly. When he opened them again, he smiled at Anise.

"I didn't know you were religious," she whispered.

"I'm not. I'm agnostic."

"You prayed just now."

"She's very observant."

"Well, why? If you're agnostic, I mean."

"I think it helps me. Sometimes. And I think it's important to say thank you."

"For what?"

"For lots of things."

"Like?"

"Like making it this far. Through the dark tunnel. And for this day. And the sun. And," he put his arm around her, "for you."

Anise thought she would melt into a puddle on the chapel floor. "Should we be kissing in here?"

"Where better?"

●●●●●

She brushed her teeth and thought of Boyd. She'd stared at the television and watched Boyd. Eaten her supper and thought of him. Walked up and down the halls and thought some more. Anise forgot to think of food and calories and her weight, thinking instead of Boyd. Got dressed for bed and remembered his eyes.

She looked at her own in the bathroom mirror. Was this really happening? To her? Anise? Was she worthy? Of his attention? Of this happiness?

Anise touched her lips that were red and plump from his kisses.

●●●●●

The next few weeks were much like a movie. A cheesy date movie, nonetheless, Anise didn't care. Dr. Z granted her her first evening pass. Boyd took her to see Shakespeare in the Park: A Midsummer Night's Dream. They visited the space science centre one weekend afternoon to stargaze in the star theatre. Mostly they just hung around the hospital grounds and gardens. Talking. About books. Boyd's favourite university profs. About movies vs. films. Music they loved. Music they hated. Anise showed him her sketchbook. Boyd was genuinely impressed.

"You could do this, you know. For a living."

"Ha! Most artists scarcely make a living."

"That's not true. Not everyone ends up a Warhol or a Miro, but there are ways to make a living—a good living—as an artist. Or a writer," he smiled at her journal which she had never yet let him see. "If you're smart. And you are, Anise."

She allowed herself to consider this. Two people she respected had now called her an artist. What if they were right?

One day she brought Boyd to the hospital school to introduce him to Rowe and Dobbins and the other students. The two teachers immediately abandoned their instruction and tripped over each other trying to be the first to shake his hand.

"So nice to meet you," both teachers gushed at once.

"Anise has told us all about you." Dobbin was grinning her fool head off.

"She has?"

"I'd just like to know what your intentions are..." Rowe with a furrowed bushy brow.

"My...? intentions?"

"Just joshin' ya! Welcome to the classroom." He clapped Boyd so heartily on the shoulder that the younger man almost lost his balance.

"Might I add that you have exceptional taste in women?" Dobbin and her big mouth.

"I do? I mean, yes, I do."

And so it went. Each moment more embarrassing than the last. At last Anise pushed Boyd out the door. He was clearly enjoying himself a little too much. "See you after school." She turned back red-faced to meet the amused eyes of her teachers. "Can we just get on with it? I mean with poetry. Please."

But it was hard to study poetry when all she wanted was to make poetry with Boyd.

she asked me to write a poem
so I thought about morning sun
through windows needing washing
and still you look gorgeous through the streaks
I wonder
how I look to you
though I know how I look to me
in this poem there is supposed to be imagery
like your reflection dancing on the water
in the pool near the park fountain

you wary and laughing beside me
then for a nano-second
I see who I am
without distortion

School was drawing to a close. Exams were next month, but that was ok. Anise's grades were honours standing, although she'd had to drop some courses. She could pick those up in the next school year or take a summer course. Ms. Dobbins and Mr. Rowe could hardly contain their delight in her. But it was sort of wonderful, too. To have such cheerleaders.

And then there was Boyd. Since they'd become an item, Anise was daring to hope. She'd gained weight. Was almost near her goal weight, in fact. She had to admit that she was feeling better. Prozac could be working. And lately Dr. Z.'s horns seemed to be receding into his head. He was...well, almost nice.

"What's that one called?" Anise stood shyly at his office door, watching him water his plants which themselves seemed healthier and more robust.

"I call him Abe. He's a prayer plant." Dr. Z.'s voice was lively. "This is Latitia. She's a jade plant. That one is Cherry although she's a miniature orange tree. And this," he spoke in reverence, "is my bonsai tree, Miko."

For the love of mike, this psychiatrist gave his plants names. Curiouser and curiouser. Downright weird. "Nice," was all Anise could think of to say.

She watched him tenderly ministering to the bonsai and reminded herself to water her lobelia. Maybe even give it a name. "Dr. Z, I have a question..." He put the watering can down and gave her his attention.

"Can someone divorce her parents?"

The psychiatrist scratched his head and cleared his throat. "Well... there is a legal action that can be taken to ensure a child is removed from a harmful situation in the home."

"No. I mean can a reasonably mature adolescent take up independent living without running away from home. Legally?"

"Yes. Some of our patients have had to do that. Under dire family circumstances. Are you considering this course of action, Anise?"

She nodded.

"Because the best thing would be family counseling so that you can reintegrate with your parents and your family upon discharge."

"I know you think that, Dr. Z. But we've tried that before. And it hasn't worked."

"Is this something to do with that young man you're seeing from 4PsychP?"

Anise watched as the nubs that had been Zeplin's horns began to protrude again. "No, Dr. Z. I'm not thinking about moving in with him, if that's what you're wondering."

He adjusted his eye glasses, several years out of fashion. "Good. Because having a boyfriend isn't the road to recovery, Anise."

Shit, she knew that. Anise flounced away into her room and continued to work on the Dr. Z charcoal studies that she had been perfecting in her sketchbook, a series she called El Diablo.

Although, of course, the thought had crossed her mind. Living with Boyd was an exciting fantasy. But that's all. There was no way she was ready for that. No way Boyd was ready. For pity's sake, they hadn't progressed further than kissing. And that was fine with her. And Boyd. For now.

But, she wondered. When wouldn't it be enough for Boyd? He was nearly five years her senior. A university student. Would he put up with a slightly terrified, sexually inexperienced high school sophomore?

And if she had her own place, wouldn't he expect the inevitable transition from kissing to full frontal nudity? And the other sexy stuff she didn't know enough about?

She closed her sketchbook and paced around her small room. It felt cramped and stuffy. If only she could leave the unit, but it was too near dinner time. Anxiety washed over her. How could she eat feeling this way? How could she eat? How could she?

For the first time in weeks she asked for a PRN to help her with the anxiety. Fran didn't bat an eye. Just led her to the little jagged pill room. Produced the tablet and gave her a paper cup of cool water.

"If you need to talk, let me know, Anise."

"Thanks."

•••••

By the time she saw Boyd again that night, she was feeling better. And she realized she needn't worry about the s-word. At least not yet. Boyd had his own stuff to work out. His own anxieties. His discharge was slated within two weeks. All of a sudden, the world seemed to him a very big, even threatening place.

"But you have a nice family to go home to..."

"Yeah. And I've let them down so many times."

"No, you haven't. You've been ill. That's not your fault." She tried not to sound like she was merely reciting the glib group therapy mantra.

"Not taking my meds was my fault. I've screwed up so often."

"You won't this time. You said so yourself. This time will be different."

"How?"

Anise swallowed. "Well... this time you have me."

"You're in here."

"Not forever."

Lu stood at the glass doors watching Anise try to cheer Boyd before he slinked off to 4PsychP to his own room. The nurse clucked her teeth at the girl's approach. "You'd better give up on that one."

"Lu, this is none of your business."

"You're my business, missy. And all I'm saying is a bi-polar boyfriend is a sure way not to get well."

"Thanks for the free advice, Lu. I'll be sure to record it in my journal."

In a huff, the nurse locked the door to the unit.

But Lu's waspish voice echoed in the girl's troubled thoughts. Each day closer to his discharge, Anise felt Boyd pulling away, retreating from her. And each day in 4-Psych-O seemed more like a prison sentence.

Chapter eleven

It's been a bad week on 4-Psych-O.

One of the youngest girls, Raylene, who's about 13 or 14 took a bottle of pain killers. They gave her that charcoal stuff, so she's okay now, I guess. But she was pretty sick.

Then a girl refused to brush her teeth because someone told her there are 30 calories in toothpaste.

Then there's Boyd.

•••••

Anise watched the little droplets of blood drip into the sink.

She considered again going to find Boyd. But he wasn't in very good shape. His state of mind had taken a small dip, or so the 4PsychP nurse had told her. He wasn't up to company. Anise swallowed that information and the accompanying lump that rose from her heart to her throat.

A few more splashes of blood.

She'd already tried to call Marcel. "The cellular customer is not available. Please call again later." He'd turned off his voice mail. So much for the brotherly support he'd promised when he gave her the damn cellphone.

More little drops of Anise in the sink. The droplets formed little rivulets. There'd be hell to pay later. But for now. Cutting was a way through this. Cutting was saving her life.

Karin's admission was the trigger, Anise knew. Karin Dartmouth. The newest inmate of 4-Psych-O. The envy of everyone. So frail she'd been brought in via wheelchair. Clearly the skinniest girl in the program. She had to weigh 44kg or less. Her presence triggered the entire ward. Set Raylene to gulping Tylenol.

I feel so fat.

She repositioned the little blade that she'd swiped from the art supplies at school. Blood was still oozing out of the first cut. She sliced again. A sigh escaped her body.

It was a kind of writing. Creative writing even. Writing on the body. Body hieroglyphics. A language only she and the Egyptians could decipher.

Dr. Z. sure as hell couldn't. Decipher Anise, that is. He was too busy drugging her up to decipher.

And Mo, Maureen, her psychologist, who really did listen, was on vacation. Nurse Fran, Anise's other ally on the ward, was at home, sick with the flu.

Too humiliated to tell the teachers at the school, Anise felt she'd be letting them down. Here she was letting everyone down. If the nurses discovered the cuts, she'd be on close and no help to Marcel. Neither could she see Boyd - they'd say she was a bad influence on him.

No one knew what Anise was writing. Feeling. And it was, after all, her story. So they could all screw off.

I know what's best for me. And it sure as hell isn't this prison.

I just need to be thin.

She took the tip of her pen and dipped it in pooling blood in the sink.

T-h-i-n.

It wasn't that she hadn't tried. She had. Even done ok for a while. Then failed. She couldn't do it. She wanted to get better. But it was so hard.

Hard to watch Liane spill ten to twenty packages of sweetener all over her supper so that she could eat it.

Hard to watch severely depressed Melinda come back from ECT dazed and stupid. There was no other word for it. Anise wondered if shock therapy was what Dr. Z. had next in mind for her. She'd bolt first.

So hard to watch her weight creep up day after day while all she felt was huge and disgusting and embarrassed by her gargantuan self.

So hard to be on constant post. Because... well, because she'd bought the diuretics. After Karin's arrival. Anise had used them. And been busted.

No one understood that it was because, in addition to Karin's presence, Niki from school had dropped by to visit and had said the h-word.

"Nise, you look so heatlthy!"

Tantamount to betrayal.

Anise loved that word. Tantamount. Used as early as 1292.

Tantamount to the f-word." Nise, you look so fat!"

Same difference.

So she'd had to do something.

And the something she did was to buy the laxative. And take it.

So now everytime she pooed, some nurse had to check it over.

So as to completely mortify me. Scatomancy. Copromancy. Scatoscopy. The nurses divine my future from my feces.

My future is shit.

·····

Maybe she should just open a vein and bleed herself. Like medieval medicine. Bleed herself into a better humour. Or just bleed herself empty. Like she already felt. Why not?

But somewhere from the deepest recesses of her cloistered self, a voice said, "No."

"No," Anise repeated. And turned on the tap water to rinse away the evidence.

Shakily, she dabbed at her wounds with a tissue. Reached for the peroxide she kept in her make up bag along with some sterile gauze bandages. Anise watched the peroxide bubble and froth up with the blood. She taped the gauze in place. Slipped the sleeve of her pajama top down over it. Finished washing out the sink. Cleaned the blade that she secreted in her make up bag.

She turned the light out and crept back into bed. Zoe was snoring softly.

If this wasn't prison, what was? Only thing missing, as far as she was concerned, were leg shackles.

Sighing, she tried to slow the images flashing across the screen of her mind.

Karin – skinny and sick and damaged, like everyone on 4-Psych-O.

Raylene – in ICU with a teddy tucked into her arms stuck with IVs.

Marcel – wounded and beyond reach while his sister was trapped in purgatory.

Boyd – terrified about his release date so self-sabotaging just prior to discharge.

GRAVITY JOURNAL

The general sorry state of the world and its six point five billion plus residents.

The other miserable inmates of 4-Psych-O.

Loathed and Witless who hadn't even been to visit since returning from their Caribbean cruise. Although they'd sent a postcard: Wish you were here. All our love. Loathed and Witless.

As if. As if they had any love left over. For her. Or Marcel. Because they were both too busy loving themselves and their money and their Manhattans and their snooty, influential friends to ever recollect that they'd sired two offspring.

Two desperate, screwed up offspring.

Anise was so tired. The sleeping pill she'd taken like a good little sick girl was beginning to take effect.

Thank god.

Or whatever.

She just wanted oblivion.

Well, if she were very honest. Maybe... just maybe she wanted something more.

Sleepily, she reached again for her journal.

Who cares about Anise?
Who cares about her heart?
Someone?
Anyone?

Chapter Twelve

"Well, Anise," Mo said, closing the cover of the girl's journal carefully and opening a manila file folder. "That has to begin with you."

"Huh?" Anise slouched in the chair opposite. Her knees were pulled up to her chest and she'd yanked her hoodie down over them. Her hands, frozen ice picks really, were secured in the black sleeves of the hoodie. It was always freezing in Mo's office. But then, Anise was always cold.

"You know what I mean, Anise. Anise has to care about Anise. Anise has to care about her own heart. First." Mo looked into Anise's eyes. "Then others will care, as well."

"Yeah. Right. Like Loathed and Witless will ever care."

"You know, you're probably right, Anise. They probably won't care. Not the way you want them to. But we don't get to pick our families do we, Anise? We are born into what we're born into. Most of us survive. Some better than others. Then in your adulthood, you build a new family."

Anise looked skeptical.

"Look, I've told you that I don't get along with my biological family, right?"

"Yeah."

"But I have great people in my life whom I consider family, Anise. Some are related, like my cousin, Hector. Others are friends I've come to know and love over the years. They're my family. The people I turn to in sorrow and need and joy and celebration. It is possible to build community. To find others with like minds and hearts and embrace them as family."

Anise shrugged. "Maybe." She thought a moment. "I have Marcel, scrambled egg that he is."

"Okay."

"And... there's Boyd."

"And there's me, the teachers. Others on your team. Maybe in time they'll become family. Maybe they'll just be supportive friends and caregivers."

Anise nodded.

"There is hope, Anise."

"You think?" She smiled shyly. "Even for me?"

"Especially for you, Anise."

"I'm glad you're back, Mo. I kind of hate it when you go on vacation."

"Yeah, well. If I didn't, there'd be a homicide on this ward." She laughed and her black braids shook. "Listen, I'll give you an emergency cell number to call next time, ok?"

Mo was looking very much like family to Anise. Although she knew about the psychologist-patient thing. Transference. Anise had looked it up. "A corollary of psychotherapy wherein the patient imbues the therapist with idealized qualities and develops feelings akin to love for the practitioner." In other words: something smarmy sort of like love that happens between needy patients and caring professionals. Still. It was good to know that Mo had her back. Very good to know.

The teachers, too. Ms. Dobbin and Mr. Elliott were so relieved to see the light back in Anise's eyes, as they phrased it. And Ms. Dobbin only said, "Thanks Anise," when she'd surrendered the exacto knife a week after her theft. No judgement. No grief. Just thanks. A wiping of the slate. Renewed trust.

There was something big to that. Renewed trust. Could Anise renew her trust? In herself? She hadn't cut for a week now. That was something.

"And another thing, Anise." Mo brought the girl's attention back to the small office decorated with African prints and colourful fabrics. "You mustn't go on thinking that you can solve everyone's problems."

"Huh?"

"You aren't the saviour of the world."

"What do you mean?"

"I mean your brother's issues and troubles, love him though you do, are not your responsibility or yours to shoulder and solve. In fact, you can't solve or own them. You won't be doing him any favours and may just enable him to keep harming himself and screwing up. Same thing with Boyd. Be his friend, but don't take on his baggage. I know that's easier said than done, especially when you've got a kind heart. But try to resist the caped crusader instinct. You've got your own closet to sort through, Anise. A lot of rooting around in your thoughts and feelings if we're ever going to lick this."

"But Marcel...Boyd... they need me."

"You need you, Anise, first and foremost. If you divert your attention always elsewhere you're never going to focus on the hard work of looking in the mirror."

"I hate mirrors."

"Of course you do. You're an anorexic." Mo shot her a gap-toothed grin and Anise smiled in spite of herself. "But you know

I'm speaking in metaphors, Miss Smarty Pants Big Words. Avoidance is your ticket for readmission to 4-Psych-O. And you know it. One last item." Mo closed Anise's thick file before her. "Your parents want to join us next Wednesday."

"Shit! No MO!"

"Yes, Anise. It may be a sign of hope..." Mo looked at the stricken girl. "Or not. But at least we have to try."

No, we don't, she wanted to yell. Hadn't she tried so many times before with her cold she-parent and ineffectual he-parent. But there was no arguing. Anise had exceeded her hour with Mo and the woman had too many other patients. The girl knew she would not win this one, so instead nodded glumly and took the sheet of questions the therapist had given her to work on over the week. Mumbled a goodbye and a thank you.

She flopped down in the psycholounge, as she and Boyd had dubbed it, and began to respond to Mo's prompts in her journal.

Losses I've suffered:

- *invasion of body – nope*
- *loss of limb – not yet*
- *loss of ability – hmmm maybe loss of ability to ever be normal*
- *loss of memory – I wish*
- *loss of sensorial perception – sometimes I feel nothing and sometimes I feel everything*
- *loss of beauty – please, as if I ever was*
- *loss of money – rich parental units, no prob there*

GRAVITY JOURNAL

- *loss of property* - I lost a filling last week - attributed to my disease and the effect on my teeth, but the hospital dentist replaced it so we're good to go
- *loss of pets* - not lately, years ago Snowy my cat got run over
- *loss of friends* - yup, none left from school, but here I have some
- *loss of home* - ha ha ha ha
- *loss of trust* - hee hee hee hee
- *loss of faith* - in our lord JC? In life? In humanity? Take your pick.
- *loss of hope* - you figure?
- *loss of love? Innocence? Identity? Past? Present? Future? Time?* - checkcheckcheck-checkcheckcheckandcheck
- *loss of boyfriend* - ?

•••••

Anise glanced around for any sign of Boyd. She met the variously empty or sad gazes of the other psych inmates. Then caught sight of wretched Alice, the elderly woman who rocked herself as though she were her own child. She felt a surge of pity for the vacant shell who must have been somebody's mother or sister or daughter some once upon time. Alice never had any visitors. What right had Anise to obsess over her own stupid troubles? The world was filled with so many more important sorrows. As if to confirm her suspicions about wading in wallowing waters, her brother burst through the door to the lounge.

Anise broke into a smile. "Mars! I'm so relieved to see you. I've been calling and calling you. Where've you been? Why isn't your voice mail activated? What's up?" And then she looked into his face.

Marcel was messed up.

"Nise! Allsorts! I need to talk to ya! Right now!" he weaved towards Anise who rose to greet him. He lurched to give her a hug, nearly knocking her slight frame to the ground.

"What the hell, Mars? What are you on?"

"Nothin'. Just a little tide-me-over. Ya know. From the rave last night."

"Marcel! You're hurting me!" She tried to free herself from his vice-grip as he dragged her to the corner of the room for some privacy.

"Look can we go somewhere? I gotta talk to you."

"No, we can't! I've got dinner in seven minutes and I can't miss a meal, Mars. You know that! If you need to talk, speak here and now. Otherwise, come back after supper for visiting hours."

"Look, Nise. I can't wait. Do you have any money?"

Anise pointed to her hospital garb. She hadn't bothered changing from her pyjamas that day at all. "Does it look like I do?"

"I mean...do you have anything in your bank account? Like a few hundred. I'll pay you back. I swear."

"What're you on, Marcel?" she looked into his bloodshot eyes. They darted from her face around the room.

"Look, you know I'm good for it, Allsorts. I'm in a bit of a bind."

"Why not ask the units? They..."

"You know I can't do that, Nise."

"Slip back into the house and..."

"I can't Nise. I can't trust them."

"They won't hurt you. They'll just give you the lecture."

"They'll send me back, Nise."

"Back where? To the Youth Detention Centre? No, they won't. You haven't done anything illegal yet..."

"I don't mean back there. I mean. They'll send me back."

"Back?"

"To Nephron."

"Huh?"

"You know. Nephron."

"No, I don't know."

"Planet Nephron. Where we came from. Before the disintegration. Before the experiments. When they stole you and me and ran with us here."

"To Earth?"

"You remember!" He beamed at his sister. "Thank god..."

"You're doing crystal meth again."

"Just give me your card and PIN..."

"Marcel, you idiot!!"

The security guard at the front desk raised his head and an eyebrow.

"Shhhh. Just a couple hundred bucks, maybe five hundred at most..."

"No way!" Anise stood suddenly. Everything shook when she spoke. "I am NOT ever giving you my bank card or my PIN number! I am going through those glass doors and I am going to sit and choke my supper down and... "

"You can't leave me hanging, Anise. I need you!"

"Any trouble here?" the uniformed security guard approached the two hissing cats in the corner.

"Leave me alone, Mars. Let go of my arm!"

"You're with them, aren't you?"

"Shut up, Marcel! You're out of your mind. And if you don't stop that shit, you'll end up in here! Get some help!"

"Fuck you, Anise!"

"Hey, buddy! That's enough. You're outta here." And with one burly gesture the security guard had Marcel by the scruff of his neck and removed him from the ward. No doubt from the hospital entirely.

Anise retrieved her journal with a shaky hand.

- *loss of brother – check.*

So much for Marcel on her team. He'd just lost his supportive family member card.

Did this qualify as taking care of her own needs first? If so, why did Anise feel like vomiting?

chapter thirteen

The next two weeks were a daze of sleeping pills and anti-anxiety and anti-nausea pills. Marcel was banned from the hospital by security, so that was one relief. Her meeting with the units was briefly postponed, so that was another. Anise swallowed med cocktails and Ensure like a good little loony. Slept through most of her days. Stared at the ceiling most of her nights. Went to group and gazed into the emptiness that was her life, all the while ignoring the other whiners talking about gagging, hating their bodies, fighting their fat, wanting to be free of 4-Psych-O. It was like a boring refrain of a bad, bad song by Britney Spears.

When the nurses forced Anise back to the hospital school, she was merely going through the motions. She couldn't retain the current date let alone the dates of the battles of WWI or the state of affairs in Iraq and Afghanistan. What she read, what the teachers said, went in and out of her brain like water through a strainer. She felt as intelligent as a crustacean. As spineless as a jellyfish.

Recognizing the futility of final exams for Anise, the teachers arranged for exemptions. Ms. Dobbin brought in the film *Frida* for her despondent student to watch over the course of the week. The life of the troubled artist flickered across the girl's lost face in the darkened viewing room. Often Anise was asleep within the first thirty minutes.

Then Mr. Rowe would put a hospital blanket over her and close the door gently.

Boyd sent her a card and a yellow rose from the hospital flower shop.

Now it was her turn not to see him. She didn't have the energy. But one evening he ventured into her room as she slipped in and out of consciousness from her somatic therapy. He sat at the bedside, held her left hand and stared at the drooping yellow head of the bud that had never opened.

One morning several days later, Anise found enough energy to put up some new magazine photos on the walls around her bed. Pics of Morrissey and Liz Phair from *Alternative Press Magazine*. Mo stopped at her doorway.

"Back from the dead, I see."

Anise shrugged.

"I'm sorry about Marcel... Have you heard how he's doing?"

"Nope."

"I brought you something. For your collection." Mo handed her a photo of a woman rolling up her right sleeve as though to show her bicep, determination set in her jaw and eyes. The slogan above her head: "We can do it!" Anise recognized the famous WWII image: Rosie the Riveter. She'd studied the poster and the movement to bring women into the workforce in Social Studies. Only recently Ms. Dobbin had brought up the image on the schoolroom computer.

Fighting anorexia was kind of like fighting a war. Waging a battle.

"Thanks, Mo." She gave the psychologist a hug. Together they hung the image on the wall nearest Anise's hospital bed pillow.

"Your parents called. Again."

"Fine. Let's get it over with."

"When?"

"As soon as possible."

"I'll set something up for tomorrow then."

"Whatever." She turned back to *AP*. Adjusted the volume of her iPod.

•••••

"People who suffer from anorexia have difficulty labeling and verbalizing internal emotional states. Suffice it to say that this meeting and the recent incidents with her brother have produced intense anxiety for Anise."

"Well, it's certainly been no picnic for us."

Anise saw Loathed adjust her three carat emerald cut diamond engagement ring. Caught her mother's blank look at the collection of signed and framed photos on Maureen Morgan's office wall: bell hooks, Angela Davis, Michaëlle Jean, Rosemary Brown, Rosa Parks.

"This has been such a trial for Trent and me. Imagine having two children who need psychiatric help."

Mo studied the three people seated before the desk in her cramped office. "I can imagine how difficult it is for you as parents. Part of why we're here is to offer the entire family counselling. I wish you'd reconsider. It's important to process—"

"WE'RE not the ones with the problems. Our children need to work on themselves. WE'RE just fine."

"Part of this illness is embedded within the family dynamic," Mo offered tactfully.

"I don't think you know anything about our family—"

"And that's part of the problem."

"Deirdre, don't you think that we should give family therapy a try?"

Anise hazarded a glance from her well-bitten nails to her father's face.

"Trent," Loathed hissed, "I'm not interested in airing any laundry, soiled or clean. Anise is the anorexic. It's her problem. Her solution. We brought her to this facility, reputedly the best in the city," this last she tossed at Mo.

Witless sat back in his chair.

"Anise has had every privilege," Loathed continued. "I just don't see why she is doing this to us."

"I'm not doing anything to you!"

"I agree, Mrs. Luther."

"It's Jasmine-Luther."

"I'm sorry... Mrs. Jasmine-Luther. But I agree. This illness is not Anise's doing, hard as that is to understand. It's not her fault. It's a symptom of feeling out of control and it's difficult to treat without getting to the root of why she feels a loss of control..."

"Take it up with her please, Miss Morgan. And good luck to you. She's always been a willful child. Despite what we've given her, what we give her, it's never enough."

"I'm never enough!" Anise's black-rimmed glare was directed straight at her mother.

"Don't be ridiculous, Anise! Have I ever said that? Have I?"

The girl dropped her eyes back to her lap and the white knuckles of her clasped hands. "No. You don't have to say it. I know it."

"Well, I don't know when you became omniscient. But you certainly have an imagination, I'll grant you that, albeit a disturbed imagination." Loathed rose to go, meek Witless close behind.

"Do what you must. Pump her with drugs. Shock her if you need. You can tell Dr. Zeplin that we'll sign any necessary papers." She clutched her clutch in her beautifully manicured talons. "Lose the melodrama and you'll be welcome home, Anise. Just don't come home fat please, dear."

Witless murmured some thanks and was out the door. All that remained was the scent of Loathed's expensive spicy perfume.

"Well, that went well." Anise grimaced. "Don't you think?"

•••••

What I don't have control over:
- *Marcel's behaviour*
- *my parents' inability to parent*
- *my weight*
- *my life*

What I'm worried about (1-10 scale):
- *Marcel's crystal meth problem – 9*
- *school next year – 7*
- *Boyd – 9*
- *sex with Boyd – 6 (right at the moment)*
- *becoming my mother – 10*
- *going home to live with the units – 11*
- *how not to go home to live with the units – 11*
- *getting fat – 11*

"Fran, I'm thinking about cutting again." Anise stood shaking in her pyjamas at the nursing station. It was 2 am.

"It's good that you're telling me, Anise. Very good. Why don't I make you some herbal tea? Would that be ok?" Fran spoke softly and led the girl gently from the desk towards the eating room. She put the kettle on to boil. Wrapped a blanket around Anise's shoulders and got the cups ready.

They took their steaming mugs into the tv lounge. Fran dimmed the lights and sat next to Anise. She took the girl's cold hand. "You're feeling desperate."

"Yeah."

"Have you tried writing in your journal? Drawing in your sketchbook?"

"Nothing's helping. Nothing." Anise began to rock back and forth. She reminded herself of Alice, the psycholounge loon. Squeezed her eyes shut against that pitiful image.

"It's ok to let out what you're feeling, Anise."

She continued rocking.

"People need to feel pain to process grief. If you allow yourself to feel the pain, maybe just maybe, you won't need to cut." Fran put her arm around Anise's shoulders. They began to shudder. And shudder.

As rain pelted the windows outside in the darkness.

Chapter fourteen

Anise's smart comeback list for the arseholes of the world (as requested by Maureen Morgan):

- to the U-Tan manager who told Tammy from the unit that she looked fat when she went in for her weekly UV shower: "I guess this is the kind of job you get when you don't finish high school."

- to the leering psych patient who proposes marriage and grabs his genitals whenever I pass by: "You've already got a wife. Your right hand."

- to my brother's girlfriend whose rejection of him triggered his current downward spiral: "Get thee to a nunnery. Oops. I mean a whorehouse, ho."

"Geez, Anise. Remind me never to piss you off," Boyd's voice was tense at her shoulder. "I thought that when you finally shared your journal with me there'd be some lovely verse celebrating my wit and intellect, my male beauty. Instead, there's this vitriolic rant page after page."

"Mo told me to write my anger out. Wring it out until I've exhausted it."

Boyd observed her pen scratching the surface of the page. "Are you really going to say all these things to these people?"

"I'm not saying. I'm writing. To deliberately seek people out and spit on them would be bad karma, Boyd."

He grinned. "Right. We don't want you coming back as a snail next time around."

- *to my brother on the occasion of his next needling of me for money: "Are we related? Because you seem familiar, but I can't recall your name..."*
- *to my father: "Get a life. Get a spine. They're one and the same thing."*
- *to my mother: "I divorce you. I divorce you. I divorce you."*

"Anything you need to tell me, Anise?" Boyd licked his lips nervously. "Because I'd rather you said it to my face and that we discuss it..."

Anise put her pen down and looked at him. Did he really want to hear what she might have to say? "Well, I didn't much like it when you shunned me during your relapse, Boyd."

"I-I was a carwreck, Anise. I didn't want you to be a casualty."

"Maybe you have to learn to trust that I can be your friend and not be dragged into your mire." Her face was hot, but it felt good to confront this issue.

Boyd gave her a two-coloured blink. "O-ok. I can work on that."

"Thank you. Because I've learned I'm not big on the whole likes-me-likes-me-not rejection thing."

"I've never stopped liking you, Anise. Ever since we first talked. Even before that...when I first saw you." Boyd touched her cheek. "And I meant what I said. I want to see you after tomorrow, when they let me out of here. I want you and me to be an us."

Anise nodded and tried not to tear up. Lately she was easily teary. This from the girl who prided herself on never crying. On drying others' tears. "There's another thing..."

He watched her face cloud over. "Give it up, then."

"I'm not ready for sex."

"O-ok."

"Maybe never."

"That's a bit harsh, Anise."

"Ok. Not yet, anyways."

"Fair enough. But I'm sure that with my boyish charm and dazzling good looks, you'll eventually be seduced..."

"Boyd! I'm serious."

"Alright, alright. I'll be serious then, too. There's no pressure, Anise. Neither of us needs that. And sex doesn't work very well at all if there's pressure. So no worries. I'm not going to push you into something you're not ready for. I respect you too much for that."

She hugged him because Anise the wordsmith could find no words to adequately express her relief and gratitude.

"I'm growing on ya, aren't I, Nise?"

"Like mould," she murmured.

•••••

They stood at the threshold of the Eliza Petraclark Memorial Hospital the following day. It was raining and cool air filtered into the foyer.

"Wish you could come with me, Anise."

"Me too," she shivered.

"Wish I could pick the lock to your prison cell and spring you free." Boyd kissed the top of her head. "Guess you're the only one with the key to unlock that door…"

"I guess."

"You've got my phone number programmed into that cellphone of yours? Groovy. Because I'm a good listener, Anise."

"Promise me you'll take your meds, Boyd." She looked up into his face.

"Promise." He bent down and kissed her. "Sealed with a kiss."

She watched him step into the rain. He stood grinning crookedly at her until his crazy hair was dripping wet.

"Get going or you'll get soaked."

"At your command, milady Anise!" He hoisted his pack onto his back and waved. She watched his tall form back away. "I'll come to visit soon, ok?"

"Ok."

"I miss your lips already!" he shouted above the patter of the rain. Only Boyd could so embarrass her. And get away with it. She watched him jog across the street towards the bus stop.

Her hands clutched the card he had given her. On the front was written in a terrible scrawl: For Anise. To be opened later.

She wandered around the hospital. Stopped at the colourful ceramic tile installation, painted by various hospital patients. Meandered through the art gallery and admired an exhibition of watercolour scenes. Paused at the water fountain and made a wish with a tossed penny.

"I'm lonely," Anise told the gushing water. And allowed the feeling to wash over her.

Her feet found their way to the interfaith chapel. She entered quietly. Behind the screens someone was praying. She sat in the pew as she and Boyd had done before, and opened his card. On the front was a photograph of a sunrise. Inside was Boyd's nearly illegible handwriting.

Anise,

Please eat. Please choose life.
I choose you.

xoox Boyd

She read it over and over. Then holding it to her breast, she whispered, "I don't know if I'm agnostic or atheist, but thanks for Boyd. Keep him well. Oh, and if it's possible, please save the world from its own self-destruction. Amen."

•••••

"Ten kilograms more and then maintenance before we even discuss this, Anise." Dr. Z. turned back to watering his bonsai.

"Ten! What do you mean ten? I'm at my goal weight right now."

"That was your goal weight. Never the medically acceptable goal weight."

"But I'm already as fat as I can stand."

"Clearly, we still have the little matter of body distortion to work on."

"Oh, and I suppose it's more drugs for that, too."

"Perhaps." Dr. Z. cut away some dead leaves from Cherry, the stupid orange tree. "We'll see how you do these next few weeks."

"Next few weeks! But I want to leave now!"

"Count on spending the summer with us, Anise."

"The entire summer!"

Dr. Z. was unfazed by her shrieking. "With occasional passes as I see fit and according to your progress and behaviour."

She stormed from the Z-devil's office. Girls and women on the unit cleared a path for her gale force down the hallway. Her bedroom door slammed with a crash that woke Karin from dreams of sugar plums two doors down. Anise looked around for something, anything to cut her flesh. But she'd discarded all sharp objects. Surrendered her nail-clippers and scissors to Fran. Shit. Just when she needed them most. Maybe she could manage a paper cut or two or a hundred...

She opened her journal.

Anise's smart comeback list for the arseholes of the world (as requested by Maureen Morgan) cont.

- *to Dr. Z. upon the occasion of raising my goal weight 10 kg — fuck you, you festering pustule of putrid humanity*

But it wasn't enough. Not nearly enough. To express her Anise anger. To exhaust it. She needed something more than words. Something better.

Incensed, she considered how to do injury to the demon spawn who was her doctor.

So she idled and she plotted, seething. Swallowed the rest of her 3600 calories and fumed. Glowered at his closed office door and strategized. Stomped the halls and kept a sullen lookout for his comb-over. Considered her counterstrike for hours.

And for hours, she didn't pee. Kept her blazing wrath bottled in her bladder. Waited. Watched for Dr. Lucifer Zeplin to quit his office for evening rounds and his final meeting with the nursing staff.

He always left his office door ajar, foolish man.

So when his room was empty and the other 4-Psych-O inmates were busy elsewhere on the ward, watching tv or playing imbecilic board games, Anise visited her vengeance. Wreaked her havoc. For his ridiculous extension of her jail sentence. And on behalf of all the other jailbirds imprisoned and force-fed in Dr. Z.'s psycho ghetto.

She closed the door in the white heat of her vexation. Anise put Miko the bonsai deliberately in the centre of the floor. Quickly unzipped her jeans and bared her bottom. Then unleashed the fury of her near-bursting bladder. With a gasp of relief, Anise whizzed all over the bonsai plant. Soaked the soil and the sphagnum moss that feathered the surface. Dribbled all over the spiky stunted needles. Shook herself dry. Zipped herself up. And left the damned plant there in the middle of the floor in a puddle of excess urine. She even thought about signing her name. Leaving a note. Your friendly neighbourhood Ureawoman.

But there had been no need for that. She could hear his screams down the hall. Dr. Z. knew immediately who the uric culprit was. And she smiled smugly to herself as she sketched in her sketchbook. Even smiled when Lu, Dr. Z.'s trusted evil assistant slapped an orange "close" band back on Anise's wrist. Smiled when the other patients gasped at and admired her audacity. Yukked it up with Boyd as she recalled the incident via cellphone late that night. Grinned when she told the story to Dobbin and Rowe, who could barely suppress their amusement, the next day at school.

In a week, she had the bracelet off and was granted an evening pass. Boyd drove her to a nearby greenhouse. She bought Dr. Z. a new bonsai. $65.00. She signed a card that said,

Here's a replacement. Call her Miko II. Your favourite patient, Anise.

She smiled sweetly as she presented the gift to Dr. Z. He accepted it quizzically but graciously. Anise chortled silently to herself and could find not an ounce of regret.

chapter fifteen

It's a pretty groovy day on 4-Psych-O. So unusual when we have one. It bears mentioning in this journal. When the inmates manage some mirth. When the nurses notice. When Dr. Z. sticks his head out of his office, sniffing in interest.

Zoe and I dressed up like the home girls we are. I'm still Allsorts from the high class hood. Zo', the farm girl from the p-diddy prairies. We donned our hippest hip hop hospital scrubs. Tied scarves around our heads. Decked out in all the bling we could scrounge between us. Practised for an hour. And then we stepped out and up for the white girls' rap performance of our lives. Plus the only rap this white girl has ever performed. I don't know about Zoe. We invited everyone to the eating room: the cleaning staff, the nurses, Dr. Z., Mo and the other psychologists, Sheila the nutritionist, the social worker, and all the patients.

Back to back we stood, Zoe and I, with our toughest faces turned to the audience. We launched into our rap ditty. I did most of the rapping, because I'd memorized the words I'd written. But Zoe outdid herself on the percussion.

GAIL SIDONIE SOBAT

A Little Medi Cocktail Rap

Well ma name is Anise
Anorexia's ma game
An I doan no

If you're wit me
But I'm telling jus' the same

I gotta have Zyprexa
Coz I gots anxietea
An' I'm nervous
An' I can't sleep
But I likes variety

So's I also take ma Prozac
Coz ma Prozac is da pill
To hep me pick ma mood up
Coz sometimes I wanna kill
Maself ya know what I mean

Ya know what I mean
Ya know what I mean
It's da medi-rap
Da liddle medi-rap
Da liddle cocktail medi-rap
A Foe Psych Oh
A Fee Fie Foe
A Foe Psych Oh

Motilium
It hep ma cilium
And ma di ges tea yon
And there's no gwes tea yon
It hep my flatulence

GRAVITY JOURNAL

But make my titties leak

So I needs Ativan
Besides my bedpan
I gots to have tham
Coz it ain't funny now
When I's a dairy cow

Sometimes I wanna kill
Maself ya know what I mean?

Ya know what I mean
Ya know what I mean
It's da medi-rap
Da liddle medi-rap
Da liddle cocktail medi-rap
A Foe Psych Oh
A Fee Fie Foe
A Foe Psych Oh

A Foe Psych Oh
A Foe Psych Oh

    They collapsed in laughter. Applauded us as we pranced about. I even did a lame fake break dance. Bruised my shoulder, but so what? Everyone cheered us on. It was exhilarating. To make them laugh. To help them take themselves with a little levity.

    Nothing wrong with a little levity mixed in with the gravity.

chapter sixteen

"Happy birthday, Anise." Zoe handed her a beanie bag lion with today's birthdate on the tag.

"Thanks, Zoe. His name is Leo. Just like my sign of the Zodiac."

"Guess you're looking forward to your birthday weekend pass."

"Yes and no. Yes, because I get out of here. No, because I have to spend the time with my hideous parents. And I may or may not see my idiot brother. I don't know what to expect if I do."

"Well," Zoe sighed, "at least your family doesn't live a province away."

"Sorry, Zo'." Anise sat beside her roommate. "I know it's hard for you to hear me talk about my dysfunctional parents and drug addict brother when you come from such a good family who love you. And can hardly ever get out here to visit you." Zoe nodded. "But just think! It's only a little longer for us both and then we're free of 4-Psych-O!"

She carried the little lion on her notebook as she and Zoe walked to school. In addition to Anise's birthday, it was the last day of classes. Rowe and Dobbin had planned a little party. A jug of Crystal Light—piña colada flavour—sat on the centre table. Sugarless gum and candies filled several bright bowls. Each girl was handed a vibrant gift bag overstuffed with colourful tissue paper. Inside were some toiletries—soaps, bubble bath, hand cream—and a candle.

"To hold you in the light," Dobbin told them solemnly.

"And this is for our birthday girl!" Rowe produced another cheerful package, as the teachers did for each of the girls' birthdays. The rumpled instructor cleared his throat importantly and began his familiar recitation a la an Oxford don: "A day of birth—also known as a birthday in the crude vernacular— is a very serious matter. One that should never be taken too lightly. Indubitably, it is an occasion for celebration," his voice was a mixture of pretension and snobbery, "but one must not assume that..."

"Ok, Guv!" Dobbin interrupted in her perfected Cockney charwoman. "That's enough, now. Let 'er get on wiv it and open the prezzie!"

"Quite so! Quite so!" Rowe acquiesced amenably.

At this invitation, Anise tore into the wrapping paper with abandon. Gasped at the contents. Inside were a set of watercolour crayons and paper and a Frida Kahlo art book. "Mylanta!" the girl gasped. "These are beautiful! Thank you soooo much!" She hugged the teachers.

The rest of the afternoon was filled with silliness and good humour. Just before school ended for the term, Dobbin produced a brass bowl with a lid while Rowe distributed little slips of paper and pencils.

"Everyone write one regret on a piece of paper."

"But I have so many," Zoe wailed.

"Just one."

Four students and two teachers bent their heads to the task. Then folded the strips and placed them in the brass bowl. Mr. Rowe lit a match.

"A little end of the year cleansing ritual. Let's burn our regrets," he announced and dropped the flame into the bowl. They stood together, silently watching the papers catch fire and curl. Ms. Dobbin held the lid ready as the flames grew. Finally, she put the lid on to extinguish them. When she lifted it again, all that remained was smoking ash.

At 3 pm, the students departed. Warm wishes for the summer months were exchanged. Anise lingered behind.

"Umm, I just wanted to tell you both... how much you mean to me. I don't know any teachers like you. Lots of days this place, this school has saved my life. So, I just wanted to thank you – for everything."

"It's been a privilege to teach you," Mr. Rowe spoke softly.

"And to learn from you," Ms. Dobbin added. "We can't wait to see the artwork you produce in your summer class... what's it called again?"

"Women Risking Art."

"Right. We want to celebrate the artistic risks you've taken when you come to visit us in the fall."

"Because," Rowe added with a broad smile, "we believe you'll be gone from this place and only return a visitor."

They each hugged Anise again. Dobbin took her by the shoulders and looked into her eyes. "While we'll be holding you in the light, you have to also hold Anise in the light. There's a great life for you out there, Anise. And you, with your sensitivity, intelligence and talent deserve to live it. You have so much to offer. Don't forget."

"I'll try not to..." Anise felt the now-familiar sting of tears at her eyes. But they weren't unhappy tears.

•••••

"Good luck, Anise," Fran called as the girl headed out the glass door of the unit alongside Mo.

"You can do this, Anise," Mo squeezed her arm reassuringly. "It's just a weekend."

"It's a test."

"In a way, yes."

"What if I fail?"

"What if you succeed?"

"But... I hate them, Mo." She turned an anguished face to the counsellor.

"Try the strategies we discussed."

"I know. I know. Go to my room and sketch or write or listen to music. Go for a walk. Watch a dvd. Practice the relaxation techniques. Meditation. Yoga."

"Stay away from your computer bookmarked evil eating disorder sites."

"Boyd is making me delete them all tonight."

"Good. Did you bring along enough Ensure?"

"Only a case of it," Anise grinned wryly. "In all my favourite flavours. And Sheila the nutritionist and I discussed food and eating strategies."

"There, you see! You're equipped with enough tips and tactics." They stood together at the front door of the hospital. "Boyd's picking you up and bringing you back?"

"For minimal contact with the units. My dad wanted to take us—Boyd, me and the two of them—out for a birthday supper. I told him no. And absolutely, under no circumstances NO CAKE! I'm not ready for that much of a risk."

"So you established some boundaries. Good." Mo gave Anise her great gap-toothed smile. "Sounds like you're set, sister!"

"What about Marcel?"

"Will you see him?"

"I don't know... He's not living at home anymore."

"Then it may not be an issue. And if it is, you can deal with it, Anise. I know you can."

"Right."

"Use the emergency number, if you need to."

Just then, Boyd pulled up to the curb in his red beater Toyota. The windows were open and Coldplay was blasting so as to wake the dead.

"Guess that's my cue."
"Sure is. Nice ride!"
"See you, Mo."
"Have a happy one, ok Anise?"

Maureen Morgan stood watching Anise put one shaky foot before the other and climb into the Toyota. With a wave and a car fart, the two psych patients peeled away.

•••••

"It's not every day you turn seventeen," Boyd chuckled as Anise admired the gold chain he'd bought her. Dangling from the centre was a small pendant that read Sunshine. He helped her with the clasp. They stood together before Anise's bedroom mirror. "Look at you!"

"What?"

"Just look at you. Here. You made it. To seventeen. And to this weekend. That's something, ya know?"

"I guess it is."

"I have another surprise for you." Boyd produced a can of lighter fluid from his backpack.

"You're going to torch the parental abode?"

"Naw! Better than that." He approached Anise's closet, paused before her bedroom window. "Getting dark out. Where are your Barbie dolls? I need your dolls."

"What the hell? Boyd is there something you need to tell me about yourself?"

"Ha ha. Very funny. Cough up the dimwit dollies."

"How do you know I have any?"

"Just a hunch. Since my sister who's older than you still has hers tucked moldering away in a basement box."

"Why do you want my dolls?"

"You'll see."

"They're in a plastic storage container in my closet."

Boyd moved to open the closet door.

"Hey! That's private! You don't just go into a girl's wardrobe, you know!"

"Then you get them for me."

"Fine."

"And while you're at it, dig out all the stupid fashion magazines you own."

A light began to dawn in Anise. "All of them?"

"All?"

"Even *Cosmo*?"

"Especially *Cosmo*."

"You just want to take the sex quiz, don't you Boyd?"

"Yeah. That's it. You're on to me now."

She handed him the plastic tub. It contained an assortment of dolls in various states of undress, hair askew, legs akimbo. Anise next searched through her piles and clutter to gather up her collection of magazines. There were roughly a hundred in total. Together she and Boyd ripped from the cream-coloured walls anything offensive or potentially triggering. What remained were some posters of bands and a Frida Kahlo painting—one of the artist's bright self-portraits—Anise had printed off from a site she'd found on the net.

"Now your weigh scale," Boyd demanded.

"I don't have one." In fact, she had a very expensive model that took very precise weight. It had been a Christmas gift. From Loathed.

"Liar."

"Not ready to surrender that."

"Now that sounds more like the truth. And that's more like it." He looked at her steadily. "Ok."

"Ok what?"

"Let's hit the fire pit in your backyard."

"How do you know anything about my backyard?"

"Quite the palace and royal gardens you live in Princess!"

Anise shrugged. "My mother comes from money. My father's in oil. They're rich. And they love being rich. It's what they love most of all. Especially my mother. But I'm serious," she pressed, "how did you know about the fire pit?"

"I scoped out your place when I found out about your birthday weekend pass."

"You could have set off the alarm system."

"Pas de problem. We locksmiths have our secret ways..."

"Sometimes Boyd," Anise shook her head, "you creep me out, you know that?"

"Ah, but you love it!"

• • • • •

Boyd doused the flames in the fire pit with more lighter fluid.

"I think that's enough, don't you? We've got a regular bonfire happening here." Anise glanced anxiously at the house, but her unaware parents were not attending.

"Okie dokie. You do the honours."

"You want me to toss my dolls into the fire?"

"That's the general idea. And your magazines, too."

"You think this will solve my little problem?" She took a doll with a broken rubber knee from the plastic tub.

"No. But it's a start. Might help, you never know. Why don't you say a little something?"

"This is too weird." But Boyd's face was earnest in the firelight. "Fine. Alright. I'll try to think of something." She looked at the doll for a moment. "Bye bye, B-doll. Had some fun times with you. But. You and K-man are such plastic friends, you know. It was all pretend with you. Make believe lives and lies."

Anise tossed the doll into the flames. Instantly the plastic began to melt. First the head and acrylic hair. Then the boobs. Arms. Legs. Impossibly thin waist and flat ass. One by one she added the other dolls. Their clothes and accessories. Ashes to ashes.

"Well?" Boyd stood watching at her side.

"That felt... good."

"Interesting. But they sure raise a stink." He covered his nose with his hand. "Let's do the mags together."

"Alright."

"You first, Anise."

She picked up a few of the fashion magazines and realized how much money she'd squandered obsessing over their photoshopped pages. "Goodbye skinny bitches!" She threw the booklets on the fire.

"Touché to that!"

Side by side, on the manicured lawn, Anise and Boyd watched the flames in the terracotta firepit gradually die down.

"You know, we burned our regrets on little slips of paper this very afternoon in the hospital school in a similar torching ritual."

"Really? And what regret did you write down?"

"I can't remember. I burned it away."

"Good on ya, Anise. You could be turning into a regular little fire starter." He tossed her playfully into the grass, leaned over her so that his ribs were touching hers. "You could set the world on fire."

•••••

Saturday was spent shopping. Loathed and Witless had given her birthday cash, so she checked out the mall. Found a few things she could tolerate and a few more at the thrift shop. And nothing in black. She'd made a promise to Mo: no more black clothes. She thought it would be a difficult promise to keep, given that her mantra had always been "I'm only wearing black until they discover a darker colour." But Anise

GRAVITY JOURNAL

found that her eye now sought out colour. Maybe it was Frida Kahlo's influence. The artist infused her work with an amazing palette of hues. Anise and Boyd had plans to watch the film about her life that evening. Her third time, his first.

Boyd picked her up to take her to the repertory movie house. She wore her new blouse, a blue peasant style with beading. They watched Salma Hayek and held hands in the darkness. Anise tried a few kernels of popcorn and Boyd made no comment.

He brought her home at a respectable hour and kissed her lightly. "Guess I'm coming for dinner tomorrow night before I take you back to the hospital."

"What did you say?"

"Dinner. A meal usually served anytime from 5 pm onwards."

"Pardon me?"

"Dinner. Or supper, if you like. Though your father expressly said 'dinner.'"

"Witless invited you?"

"He did."

"Omigod."

Five things to tell your fear:

1. *Go away anxiety. They are not going to give him the third degree. I will be able to swallow my food. And if I can't, I'll drink Ensure while they gorge on filet mignon.*

2. *Stop it worry. They are not going to ask about his parents' income. I can divert the conversation, if necessary.*

3. *Beat it dread. They are not going to ask about his aspirations or judge him negatively because he is not in the Faculty of Business. I will*

coach him beforehand not to mention his ambition to collect seashells for a living in Baha.

4. Piss off self-doubt. They are not going to humiliate me. They are not going to humiliate me. They are not.

5. Fuck off terror. Remember: they are not my real parents. They are from the planet Nephron. And they can't hurt me...

Her bag was packed and sat expectantly on the fine Asian carpet, awaiting escape by the front door. A quarter hour had ticked by and there had been no catastrophes in the grand dining room. Anise's maternal grandfather, a slight frown pursing his lips, presided over them all from his portrait above the elegant fireplace. Boyd was holding his own with Witless in conversation about golf and Mike Weir. But Anise shuddered whenever she looked at her mother. Though Loathed appeared to be politely listening, merely sipping her wine at intervals, Anise knew she was sizing up her boyfriend. As if sensing this, Boyd turned his odd-coloured eyes on the hostess.

"Your dining room looks beautiful Mrs. Jasmine-Luther."

"Please Boyd," Witless chortled, "call us Trent and Deirdre."

Her mother smiled thinly. "Thank you Boyd. This was my grandmother's pattern. We thought it being a special occasion and all..."

Anise held her breath as Boyd picked up the Wedgwood bread plate to examine it more closely. But he managed to put it down without mishap.

"You're five years older than Anise, is that so?"

Anise blurted, "Not quite five."

"Your daughter is much older than her years. Wise."

"Too wise, it often seems." Loathed set down her claret glass carefully. "What is it your parents do for a living?" Her mother dabbed at a corner of her painted mouth with a white napkin.

Boyd had just taken a hearty mouthful. There was an awkward moment while everyone waited for him to swallow.

"My dad's a locksmith. My mom's an accounts clerk. Pretty average people."

"A locksmith. How interesting." Loathed, touching her pearls, positively gloated.

"Yes, Mother. Boyd's dad could break into your home and steal everything you own. Even this fine china and heirloom silverware. Grandmother's pearl necklace around your neck. If he wanted to."

Boyd stifled a chuckle.

"Really, Anise. There's no need to be nasty. I'm just interested in Boyd's background."

"Of course you are," Anise said under her breath.

"And you're studying comparative literature at the local university, aren't you?"

Boyd nodded, "On full scholarship."

Anise barely managed to swallow her sip of Ensure. Vanilla. The least offensive flavour.

"Are you planning to go on after your arts degree?" Loathed was relentless, "To graduate school at another university perhaps?"

"I don't really know, Mrs. Jasmine-Luther. I've got to take it one year at a time."

"Because of your illness."

Anise gawped at the velociraptor who was her mother.

But Boyd was cool. "Yes. But there's also the matter of money. I have to work and save up for my tuition. Apply for more scholarships.

My parents help, but they're of modest means. And I'd rather not go into serious debt with student loans."

"Of course, not. That's very level-headed on your part." Loathed gave him her best reptilian smile. Then leapt at Boyd's exposed throat. "It's manic-depression, isn't it? That you suffer from."

Anise actually felt her heart stop pumping, the life draining from her.

But Boyd's reply was interrupted by a bursting through the door. An unkempt interloper stumbled into the grand dining room to defibrillate her heartbeat.

"Hey Ma! Hey Pa! Oh hi, Sis! And new guy!"

Mars. Higher than Pluto.

Witless rose from the table to approach his son.

Loathed screeched most unbecomingly, "Marcel, we made it clear that you are not welcome in this home under the influence of that drug."

Her brother was wild-eyed and shaking. He pointed at Loathed. "You! You're the reason. You devour your own young. Stay away from me!"

"Be sensible, son," Witless tried.

"Dad! Dad man. I just need a little cash, ok?"

His father reached for his wallet.

"Trent, I forbid you to give that boy a cent!" Loathed moved towards the pair.

Suddenly, Anise felt she was watching a film in slow motion. Marcel grabbed his father's wallet and turned to go. Loathed shrieked in protest. Witless grabbed his son's bedraggled, soiled jacket. Marcel turned around swinging and his clenched fist just missed his father's jaw. A volley of obscenities. Then Marcel pulled free and was gone from the house as time resumed real speed.

"Anise, we should go," Boyd said softly at her ear.

They said quick goodbyes to her shaken father. Loathed had already made a cool retreat from the dining room.

Boyd drove in silence. Finally, Anise said, "Sorry for the circus."

"No need to apologize."

"Yes, I do. For my mother. She's so class-conscious." Anise bit her lip. "And the private stuff she brought up... she probably phoned the unit and Dr. Z. to find out all about you."

"It's ok."

"I'm so ashamed."

"I feel sorry for them."

"I- I don't know if I can live there again."

"It must be hard."

"Like living in a deep freeze."

chapter seventeen

"While you were gone these two guys, Davey and Curtis, came into the program," Zoe gushed. "And all the girls were hanging around sniffing their butts. You know 'cause guys are so rare in 4-Psych-O. And Jolene-Big-Boobs-in-Everyone's-Face was saying how Davey was hot and definitely into her.

"Then Dr. Z. put the guys into a room together, you know. Because Garth, the other guy on the unit, is way too old, not to mention too weird to make a good roommate. Davey and Curtis were perfect strangers. But not for long because it turns out they're into each other, if you know what I mean. And they were making out in the tv room and doing it at night."

"So what happened?" Anise stopped unpacking her bag.

"Well, Lu caught them kind of red-handed, if you get my drift. And they were marched individually into Dr. Z's office. He separated them pronto and put Curtis into Garth's room after all."

"But Garth's such a rabid homophobe!"

"Uh huh. So Curtis already hates him. And then there's Rasheema who told us all that she is pregnant and will be going on mat-leave in the fall, so you were right. She's not just packing on the pounds and I owe you five bucks."

"Wow! Sounds like an eventful weekend. Anything else interesting happen?"

"I'm going home next week."

"Oh, Zoe! That's great news!" Anise hugged her. Secretly, she dreaded the thought. Zoe was her friend. An ally. Now a brand new skeletal misfit would take Zoe's empty bed within hours. There was a waiting list to get into the program. An endless list of skinny, sick girls and lately more stickmen guys.

Anise would have to forge a new relationship with a complete stranger. Someone who might spark her own insecurities, although Mo insisted that Anise was the boss of herself and her triggers. Aloud, she told Zoe, "I'm happy for you. It's time. You're ready."

She and Zoe exchanged e-mail addresses and promised to write and stay in touch. Anise gave her a watercolour she'd painted as a parting gift. She helped Zoe pack and then helped her cheerful parents load her bags into their truck. Zoe drove way and Katyana moved in.

Doe-eyed, frail, raven-haired Katyana. Who wept all night and most of the day. Whose parents were immigrants and expected their beautiful girl to behave as though she were still living in their traditional culture. Insisted that she study her mother language—Serbo-Croatian—while maintaining honours grades and working after school in their store. That she then go to university, meet a nice boy and marry within the faith and culture. Never under any circumstances was she to date a Canadian boy. She was to always unquestioningly obey her parents and abide by their strict rules. She was suffocating. She was dying.

Katyana spilled all of this in the span of only a few hours on the third evening after her arrival. Anise marveled at the girl's ability to share her problems so freely.

"You are a good listener, Anise. Thank you." Finally, her roommate drifted off to sleep.

Anise felt drained. She might be a good listener, but it was too much to process. She turned on her reading light and flipped open her journal.

So many kinds of parents. Zoe's who are loving and supportive. Katyana's who are dictatorial and rigid. Mine who embody inefficacy and frigidity. You have to have a licence for so many things: driving a car, marriage, even fishing, for the love of mike. Why not parenting?

And why with so many kinds of parents, even good ones, are we all in this prison?

•••••

She asked Mo the question during their post-weekend de-briefing session.

"Eating disorders are a complex group of illnesses, Anise. Even professionals don't have the answers. You'd think someone like Zoe, with everything going for her—intelligence, a supportive family—would be fine. Maybe she started dieting; it's the common trigger denominator in almost all patients' lives, after all. She might have had a genetic predisposition. A biochemical or hormonal imbalance. Then there are those who buy into the cultural messages that abound and bombard us millions of times a day."

Anise nodded. Like Vicki who was notorious on the ward. A fashion tv addict. The nurses had made her throw out her fashion magazines—greater numbers than even Anise had accumulated—because they were negatively affecting the other girls and women on the ward. Vicki'd had breast implants and a nose job. Her skin was tanned to a deep brown. Her hair extensions and acrylic nails were the envy of many. She longed to be Paris Hilton, only skinnier.

"Too many girls and women fall in love with their disorder because they think it is the only thing that defines them or sets them apart as special. If they give up the anorexia, who will they be?"

Anise had wondered the same thing sometimes.

"Others suffered a childhood trauma, sometimes but not always sexual; some were the victims of intense bullying or cruelty. The disease offers them an illusion of control. Still others don't want to grow up and anorexia arrests the maturation process, though at great risk to their health. Staying forever a girl, never a woman, can be a very attractive option when the adult world appears dangerous and difficult."

"And then there's me. I should be happy."

"Who says?"

"I'm so lucky. Privileged. And these are the best years of my life... all that crap."

"It is crap. Adolescence is a very challenging time for almost everyone. It was painful and hideous for me."

"It was?"

"Sure. I was a plump, black girl in a mostly white and racist town. But I survived. Like the song by Gloria Gaynor." Mo gave a hearty laugh. "I believe I've triumphed over all that small town ugliness. I don't feel I'm on the outside looking in any longer. Got me some great friends, colleagues I respect. Even some excellent patients." There was mischief in her wink. "And I'm not plump, but curvaceous."

Noticing that her hour was up, Anise rose to go. Mo handed her a paper. It was a brightly coloured Certificate of Bravery.

"What's this?"

"Exactly what it says. You passed the test. Your weight didn't fluctuate. You didn't cut or in any other way self-destruct. You made it through a difficult trial weekend. Congrats!"

Anise posted the certificate above her bed that night, right beside Rosie the Riveter.

GRAVITY JOURNAL

Katyana had been an hour in the bathroom. Anise had heard her purging. She adjusted her earphones and searched her iPod for Gloria Gaynor, turned to a fresh page in her journal and began to write:

brave – having or showing courage, especially when facing danger, difficulty or pain

brava – a shout of approval for a woman or girl performer

Brava

> today
> I make the brave choice
> not to cut
> not cut up
> my legs my arms my face my body
> for some
> someone else's
> miss-rendered notion
> of beauty
> I know that no matter
> how many knives
> cut to the chase
> such pursuit in the end
> must be at last lost

chapter eighteen

"Women have been burned for daring to make art. For taking artistic risks."

Is that true, Anise wondered? She scribbled in her notebook. Something to research later. She glanced up at the wild-haired woman, Camilla de Branscoville, before her. Draped in an artist's smock, the creature whirled dervish-like about the artroom of the community centre, only stopping briefly to stare into the faces of each of the eight women in the class.

"Or they've died trying to make art. Ergo—" She twirled again to send a smouldering look directly at Anise, the youngest member of the class. "Art is risky business. So exactly what are you prepared to risk, hmmm?"

The woman was clearly mad.

"Umm..." Anise began.

"It's a rhetorical question... for now!" She breezed over to the paper on the easel at the front of the room. Identical to the other eight easels before each of the art students in the circle. "We are going to risk, in a variety of media—paint, pastel, charcoal, text, fabric, clay, paper mache, multi-media—making art. We're going to write the woman's body, write on the woman's body, write the body beautiful. We're going to dare..." Camilla was building to a crescendo now, "we eight happy women, to make women's art! Molly, if you please." From behind a screen, she summoned forth a woman in a dressing gown. Without hesitation, the model slipped from the gown and into position on the green fabric draped over several wooden crates in the centre of the students' circle.

Anise tried not to gasp. The woman, perhaps in her thirties or forties, was utterly unabashed. And she was not in any way what one could call slim. In fact, she had fleshy thighs. A rounded paunch of a tummy. Ample buttocks. Large nipples on breasts of two different sizes. Cellulite.

Camilla instructed Molly to take an initial sitting pose, and adjusted the light on the woman. Dreamily, the instructor turned to the class. "Now, begin!"

Eight hands reached for the charcoal before them and did as told. Anise sketched for perhaps ten minutes. Camilla instructed Molly to change her pose. Papers were flipped over the easels. The model stood. The artists sketched. Camilla flitted about the room. Her suggestions were at best minor. She told Anise to observe the lines. Time ticked by.

Anise glanced over at the other artists. Clearly some were ahead of her in skill and ability. Others were struggling to make anything at all of the exercise. She repeated the mantra she'd invented to help cope with anxiety over this class. "I don't have to be perfect. I don't have to be perfect. I don't have to be..."

At the end of two hours, each of the students had a number of studies of the model. They were instructed to take these home and do something with one of them.

Anise rolled up her papers in bafflement. What something could she do with these charcoal scratches?

She puzzled on the walk back to the hospital. Over supper. In her room. There was only one sketch from the afternoon, the second last, that she thought was in any way worthy of something.

"Katyana?"

Her roommate looked up from the fashion magazine, forbidden on the ward, that she was reading. "Huh?"

"Do you have any old mags I can cut up?"

"Sure," Katyana smiled, eager to help. She reached for a gym bag under her bed. Unzipped it to reveal perhaps two dozen magazines. "Any of these."

Anise took a breath and picked up her scissors. Forced herself to look at the images as an artist. To make artistic selections. She cut out eyes, ears, feet. Lips, necks, toes. Belly buttons, shoulder blades, knee caps. And she began to arrange and paste these on the charcoal sketch.

"An interesting pastiche," was Camilla's abbreviated comment. "You must read Adrienne Rich." And the woman swept over to the next student.

Anise carefully recorded the name in her journal. Then she picked up the paintbrush and studied the new model, Maxine, a towering big-boned Amazon who looked as though she played for the local women's rugby team. Or perhaps the men's team. Struggling to capture the woman's angles, Anise dashed through nearly her entire stack of paper. Her Picasso-esque effort, several days of work later, earned a nod from Camilla.

The students were next invited to say something in the following week of classes when they moved to sculpture. Some took that literally, introducing their pieces at length, only to meet with de Branscoville's scorn. Anise took chicken bones from one of the hospital meals, boiled and arranged them like vertebrae on a black fabric background. She called it *Getting a Backbone*. Camilla rewarded her with a tight smile.

Obviously, there was no pleasing the woman. She gave at most a curt "good," a recalcitrant "carry on." Anise had paid for the course with her own money. All she could do was soldier onwards. At least she was thinking about the course more than her weight or her own body. Or her own body as it gained weight. It was good to have something else to obsess over.

Colour was the focus of the following week. Something to do with risk and colour. No matter what medium. Anise carefully simulated an abstract stained glass window in vibrant acrylic colours. Then she asked Dr. Z. if she could revisit her charts from her admission to current day. It was a big risk. But that's what she was being invited to do, wasn't it? Again she did her best to don her artist's objective hat and eyes. She sat in his office and carefully noted her weekly weights for the duration of her hospital stay to present. Then on each of the stained glass coloured pieces, she stenciled the various weights in random order: 44kg, 53kg, 49 kg, 43kg, 57kg and so on. Anise called the piece *Painting by Numbers* and it garnered a raised de Branscoville eyebrow.

For her paper mache sculpture of a woman writhing in agony, based on sketches of the newest model, Lila, Anise coated a figure with newspaper headlines about women in Afganistan, in Darfur, in Congo, China and India who endured human rights abuses. Camilla revisited it three times, finally pronouncing it "successful."

Then the instructor dropped the artistic bomb. The women artists were to spend the following three-day interim depicting themselves, preferably nude. Anise trudged back to the hospital, dismayed. Thought seriously about dropping the course. Spent a sleepless night tossing in sweat and anxiety. Talked to Mo.

Finally, late at night, she entered the bathroom, sketchbook in hand. She locked the door. Slipped off her pajamas. In the harsh fluorescent light, it all looked worse than she'd imagined. It was too much.

This class. This assignment. This body. Anise slumped to the floor and wept.

Eventually, she fell asleep on the floor of the can. Katyana's frightened knocking roused her at six am, the morning of the art class. Anise dressed herself. Did a rough sketch of the inside of her elbow, *The Crook of My Arm*, and slumped into class. She couldn't meet Camilla's eyes. But the woman said nothing and passed on. Anise breathed a sigh of relief.

There was nothing to do but continue to try. From the table strewn with thrift shop and landfill articles that Camilla had brought in to class, Anise selected an old window frame. She sanded and primed it, finally coating it with sky blue paint. Over the weekend, she attached a background and in each of the nine panes, handwrote the lines of her poem, Brava. She was invited to read the piece aloud, and the class applauded.

Boyd admired the window pane later that day. Helped her to mount it on her hospital bedroom wall. "Wow. Anise. You write. You paint. You sculpt. Is there anything you can't do?"

"Eat a cheese pizza," she managed to laugh.

The remaining weeks of the course were to be spent working on the final project in which the women had to take what Camilla termed a profoundly personal artistic risk.

Anise tried not to panic. Resisted the urge to abandon the course. Or to purge. Instead she took her meds. Patiently she sketched. Experimented with paints. Jotted in her journal. Tried not to remember how she looked in the mirror.

chapter nineteen

"Move your fat ass!"

"That's the moment you identify as the beginning of your eating disorder?" Mo scribbled in her notes.

"Yes. Rick Currie, the cutest and most popular guy in junior high said that to me, a grade eight nothing, because I was standing in the way of his locker. I'd never really thought about it before. My ass. But suddenly it became the most significant thing in my life."

"You began to diet."

Anise nodded and took a sip of her diet Sprite. "I'd always been a picky eater. So it was easy. I found I was good at it. Dieting and exercising. Really, really good.

"I got lots of positive feedback. Friends at school noticed my weight drop and congratulated and envied me. My mother, who is herself rail thin like my grandmother, encouraged what she termed my 'careful eating habits.' She is somewhat fat phobic. Has no respect for those who can't control their eating. Thinks that anyone fat or obese is clearly lazy and not terribly bright. So I had all that going for me.

"Only when I collapsed at school and had to be taken via ambulance for my first hospitalization did anyone really recognize I had a problem. You're so celebrated if you're thin. What could possibly be wrong?"

"And once you gained weight during hospitalization?"

"I was released early. I didn't get to maintenance. And I went immediately back to my old patterns. It was around that time that I began cutting."

"Do you know why, Anise?"

"I'd heard about it from other girls on the unit." Anise began winding a strand of dark hair about her index finger. "I pretty much hated my life. By then my relationship with my parents was in the sewer. Marcel was faring no better with them. So he became my ally. We used to plot a bloodless coup so that we could take over our lives. And at night I would stage my own bloody revolution with the razor blade."

"Did you ever turn to any friends?"

"I didn't really have any friends at school, just Niki. Who is pretty fickle and shallow. Most lunchtimes I'd spend hiding in a cubicle in the can. I felt like I was always standing at the sidelines looking in on the lives of other high school students. A spectator. Some of them are just so…so stupid, you know? But the truth is, I would have liked to participate, if I'd been invited."

She unloosed the tendril from her finger. "But I wasn't. So Marcel was it. My comrade and confidant. Until lately."

"Pretty lonely out there on the margins, isn't it, Anise?"

"I guess you understand that, huh Mo?"

"And how about these days? Do you have friends now that you're nearing the end of your time in the hospital?"

"Well, there's Boyd. We hang out quite a bit together. I still stay in touch with Zoe. Lately, I've been chilling with E.D.; we have a similar dark sense of humour and she's smart. She's also from the city here and interested in some of the same things: we're going to volunteer together at the Global Visions Film festival. My new roomie, Katyana is ok, but she's needy and she purges, so I try to keep a healthy distance."

"Good for you. Now that you're at your goal weight, how do you feel?"

"Like I'm fat, but ok. I'm dealing better with it. I think I can maintain. But I'm worried that I'll get fatter."

"We'll keep working on those body image issues, ok? Are you talking with Sheila?"

"Yeah. She's been designing a nutritional plan with me."

"You've got another weekend pass coming up."

"Yeah." Anise's voice was flat.

"So we're on track for your discharge later this month."

"I guess. But Mo," Anise swallowed, "is it normal not to want to go home?"

•••••

Her horoscope for August 7th: "Resist the urge to wear your heart on your sleeve."

Hadn't she been doing exactly that for seventeen years? Her entire screwed-up existence? Hadn't that resistance led to cutting? Led to 4-Psych-O?

Anise turned the page of the newspaper. At least she wasn't on the obit page. Yet. That was good news.

And then a hot white flash before her eyes. Anise blinked. And again. And gulped. She took a sip of her diet vanilla Coke in a vain attempt to swallow the lump forming in her throat. She resisted the gag impulse and, not daring to breathe, read silently: "Ivana Cassidy, 30 of Okotoks, AB, after a brave fight, succumbed to a lengthy illness. Beloved daughter of Nessie and Joe Cassidy of Okotoks, sister to Joe Jr.

and Priscilla of Calgary, AB. Funeral Saturday, August 12th, 4:00 pm at Scarboro United Church, Calgary, AB."

An image of Ivana, her protruding ribs as she bent over her meal and attacked it with spices. Ivana chronically anorectic. Institutionalized Ivana. Ivana in a wheelchair, being spoonfed.

Ivana who'd gone AWOL from the unit and the hospital only a couple of weeks ago. She'd not returned from a weekend pass. The matter had not been discussed by the staff with the patients. All very hush hush. As though Ivana had just ceased to be. But the patients had done plenty of talking amongst themselves.

"Maybe she met a guy," Vicki offered.

"Naw." Karin shook her head in disbelief. "I'll bet she entered another program. Like she did once before."

"Or maybe she finally just had enough..." Raylene sniffed.

And, of course, it seemed she had. Or her body had.

Ivana could just as easily have been her, be her. Anise. She could be the next dead anorexic girl.

The heart that she was not to wear on her sleeve split open. Anise began to cry.

Her tears spilled across the newspaper, smudging the print. She cried for Ivana. She cried for Katyana. She cried for Raylene. Helen and Karin. Vicki. Zoe. E.D. And she cried for herself. All the other girls struggling with this illness. And guys. For all of their lost hearts. All of their hungry hearts locked tightly, tightly away.

● ● ● ● ●

Boyd drove her home from Calgary and the funeral. They'd spent the night at his Aunt Kerry's. Most of Anise's weekend pass was being used up on death.

The funeral had been a grueling affair. Ivana had been cremated, so there was no coffin or open casket. Thank god. A photograph of Ivana, thin and ethereal but clearly in her earlier stage of the illness, sat upon the altar. Flowers gave off a sickening fragrance. Anise and Boyd sat with several nurses, Fran among them, who'd also come down for the service. Dr. Z. was nowhere to be seen in the great wooden building.

After the family took their seats, the ceremonies began. The Scarboro choir sang "Amazing Grace," one of Ivana's favourite hymns. She had been a chorister before her illness prevented her from singing. Several people spoke about Ivana's always cheery presence in the community, and her uncle delivered the eulogy. Anise did not recognize the little girl he described: a child full of hope and energy. The kindly minister spoke of peace for Ivana. Anise certainly hoped so, given the years of misery the young woman had suffered. By the time the choir began "The Prayer," everyone was reaching for Kleenex.

A reception was held in the church basement after the service. Ivana's parents were tearful and greeted guests shakily. Anise introduced herself as a friend from the program and Mrs. Cassidy grasped her hand tightly. "Thank you for coming, dear."

Anise overheard a relative whisper that Ivana's ashes would be scattered later, in a private family ceremony, over the Bow Falls in the Rocky Mountains. There seemed little else to do but say quiet goodbyes and leave. Before she did, Anise dropped off her sympathy card with its donation to the Eating Disorder Awareness Society, as the family had requested.

And that was it. A young life was over. A flower budded but never blossomed. Or so it seemed to Anise who thought carefully about her own life on the journey homeward.

• • • • •

When Boyd dropped her off at home, it was quite late at night. Loathed was sitting in the living room, a book in hand.

"How was the funeral, dear?"

"How do you think it was, Mother?"

"Terribly sad, I'm sure."

Anise left her and climbed the long stairway, heading towards her room. She threw open her door and gasped.

Everything had been changed.

Her room had been repainted a cautious mixture of rose and taupe. There was no sign of her posters or the Frida Kahlo. The bed, a new Queen size, was draped in some dreadful floral print instead of her old twin bedspread of Edvard Munsch's *The Scream*, which she had saved for and purchased herself. Her desk had been swept clear but for her laptop. She rummaged at the back of the desk and found her several USB data keys that she'd secreted with tape to the back. Anise flew to her closet and walked into a near-empty vault. All that remained were her winter coat, a few pairs of shoes and boots. In her drawers, entirely new sets of underwear with tags from La Senza still attached. Her toys, cherished and hoarded for years, were all disappeared.

Anise's wounded animal yelp brought her ice queen mother to the bedroom door.

"What's wrong?"

"What have you done?"

"What does it look like we've done? We've redecorated on behalf of your coming home. We took your cue from your discarded doll trunk of two weeks ago. Don't you like it?"

"NO! Why did you...? Why didn't you consult me about this?"

"We consulted an interior decorator. I think she did an excellent job. And you can shop for an entirely new wardrobe. I thought you'd appreciate that. Getting rid of the old. In with the new."

"How could you violate my room?"

"Calm down, Anise!"

"I will NOT calm down. You had NO right!"

"In fact," her mother's voice took on its customary oppositional chill, "we had every right. This is, after all, our house."

"Where are my toys?"

"Given to Good Will."

"Get out!"

"Pardon me?"

"Get OUT!" Her mother stood dumbly still. "I said GET OUT OF MY ROOM!"

Something in her daughter's raging eye persuaded the woman to back away. Anise slammed the door in Loathed's face.

With a shaky finger, she dialed Mo's emergency number.

"Mo, I think I'm gonna cut."

"Anise! What's wrong?"

The girl told her. About Ivana's funeral. About the rape of her privacy. "I'm afraid I'll cut and cut and never stop."

"Hold on, Anise! Listen, there's a good side to your anger. Strength is emoting! Remember! Don't be disconnected with what's bothering you. Find a constructive way to express your resentment and hurt."

"Like ripping out her eyes? Driving a stake through her heart?"

Mo half-chuckled. "Metaphorically speaking."

Anise took a deep breath.

"Good. Breathing is good, Anise. Keep breathing."

"Ok."

"Now promise me that if you feel like cutting or purging or worse, you'll call again, no matter the time. Alright, Anise?"

"Promise."

•••••

Witless knocked softly at her door a few minutes later. Anise cracked it open.

"I heard you and your mother had a little... altercation."

"You could say that."
"Your mother only wants the best for you, Anise."
"Right."
"I think you owe her an apology."
"I'm going to bed."
"In the morning then."

Anise closed the door on her paternal unit. She sat cross-legged on the floor, thinking and waiting. It wasn't long before she discerned the soft click of her parents' bedroom lock. She sighed audibly. Slipped on warmer clothes and her hoodie from her pack. Stuffed her laptop, her mini-printer and the rescued data transfer keys into her bag. Slinked out her bedroom door and down the stairs. All the way to the basement. Clicked on the light.

There they were. Tucked into a corner shelf of the storage room. Forgotten or ignored by her purging parents. The family of dolls in the expensive dollhouse ordered from England, replete with tiny handmade and expensive reproductions of period furniture. She pulled out the mommy and daddy dolls, the Anise and Marcel dolls.

At her father's tidy workbench, she located two paint stir sticks and lashed them together with twine. She found a black sharpie permanent ink pen and stuck it in her jeans' pocket.

Anise grabbed a flashlight, mounted the stairs and tiptoed to the back deck door. She slid it open, then traipsed down the several levels of the immaculate deck and over to the garden shed. Here she located a small spade and wandered over to her mother's flower bed, the showcase rose garden visible from the kitchen nook window.

Taking great care not to disturb the roses' roots, she dug a foot-deep hole. Into this earthen pit she dropped the daddy doll and the mommy. She thought carefully about the Marcel and Anise dolls, but in the end, she dropped these in, too. Anise filled the grave.

She planted the paint sticks at the site and snipped a single white rose from the nearby bush. This she placed under the cross that read in Anise's neat script: R.I.P.

Moments later she passed beneath the streetlamps of her exclusive neighbourhood, padding quietly through the emptied, tree-lined streets. She thought of calling a cab, but decided to save her money. Sometime in the middle of the night, she wandered into a Tim Horton's, ordered coffee and wrote until dawn. Then she called Boyd and afterwards Mo. Gave them both the same message.

"I've buried my family in a shallow grave."

chapter Twenty

Corpse

the afternoon of the day I was admitted
some humanunkind
pasted a photo of a corpse on my lucky 13 locker
a fitting tribute
to what I was fast becoming

I've buried a friend
a family
my anger
my hunger for so long
I can't remember the colour of hope

lately I sense the gravity gravitas
of a deathwish for an early grave...

Chapter twenty-one

Her cell phone rang.

She reached for it in the darkness. Boyd was out of town visiting relatives. Maybe he was calling out of late-night boredom.

But it was Marcel's name on the call display. She opened the bedside table drawer and dropped the phone inside. Closed the drawer. Then Anise turned over in her hospital bed and slipped back into medicated dreams. Eventually the ringing stopped.

In the morning, she ignored her brother's text message: "Nise. Call me."

Several weeks had dribbled by since the weekend of the funeral and the redecorating discovery. Despite weak protests from her father, Anise refused to meet again with her parents. In all this time, Marcel had never called her or returned her calls. Well, now she was busy. Getting her act together. Registering for classes in the fall so that she could finish high school. Looking for a part-time job. Finding a new path. A new home.

Mo had arranged an appointment for her with a community social worker. Together they were beginning the process of moving Anise permanently from the parental abode. There was, she was daring to believe, a life to be lived after 4-Psych-O.

The meeting took most of the morning as forms were filled out, questions were asked, Dr. Z. was consulted. Followed by telephone calls to various social services on her behalf. More questions. More forms faxed and re-faxed. By noon Anise was exhausted.

Her lunch was interrupted by Fran, who called her out of the eating room and into the dispensary.

"Anise," she shuffled uncomfortably from foot to foot. "I have... some bad news. About your brother." Fran steadied herself and looked at the girl. "He-he's taken an overdose."

"Where is he?" A chill began in her toes and worked up her legs towards her torso, touching her heart.

"In ICU here in the Eliza P. Hospital."

"I've got to see him." She turned to go, but Fran caught her wrist.

"Anise! Do you really think...?"

"Fran. I'm going. To see my brother. Marcel."

She shook herself free.

And ran from the unit. Through labyrinthine corridors and down stairs. A rat in a sterile maze. Past the halls of the hopeless and hopeful and delusional. Heedless of the sick, the sicker and the dying. Finally, she reached the doors of the Intensive Care Unit. Banged on the glass.

A nurse within signaled her to pick up the nearby phone.

"Yes, can I help you?" Anise could see the nurse behind the glass, speaking into the telephone.

"I've come to see my brother," she barked into the receiver, "Marcel Luther."

The nurse checked her clipboard. "Are you a family member?"

"I'm his sister. I-I'm also a patient here." Anise held up her wrist so that the nurse could see her hospital bracelet.

"Alright. I'll buzz you in. You'll have to put on a gown and mask. Wash your hands thoroughly..."

"Yes, yes. Just let me in. Please."

•••••

She sat in silence at his emaciated side. Loathed and Witless had just left. Her father's face awash in misery; her mother's sheer shellac. Anise had said nothing to either. Just listened to the undertones of explanation.

According to the emergency medical personnel who'd brought him in, Marcel had been tweaking on crystal meth, apparently for several days. He had been smoking and injecting along with other user friends when he had suddenly freaked out. Overcome by a wild, uncontrollable rage, he'd tried to throttle one of his meth buddies, but in the process had succumbed to violent convulsions. Someone had the presence of mind to call 911. By the time the ambulance had arrived, Marcel was comatose. He'd suffered a stroke.

There was no sure way to know what kind of permanent damage he'd done to his brain.

Tears pricked at Anise's eyes. "You fuck-up!" she murmured. Marcel's stone-still face was marked with scratches. He'd been trying to dislodge insects or worms that he'd hallucinated were attacking him. An odor of the drug emanated from his body. IV lines and a heart monitor were attached to her brother. Marcel, a broken doll.

What kind of sister was she? Why hadn't she answered the cell phone? Why hadn't she returned his call? Why had she failed him?

Why did she continue to fail? Everyone and everything. She was the one who should be lying there. Anise. Not beautiful and talented Marcel. She was the cutter. The anorexic freak. The loser. The lost cause. Her brother didn't deserve this fate. Anise did.

In a turmoil, frantic dark thoughts turned somersaults in her troubled head. Anise begged Marcel to wake up. She bargained with the powers to help him regain his health. Not to be brain damaged. To kick this repulsive habit. If he lived. If only he lived.

She stared at the shell of her brother. No movement in his body. Behind his eyes. Maybe he was brain dead. If so, Anise couldn't live with that. She was to blame.

After some hours, and at the urging of the ICU staff, she roused herself. Tore off the paper gown and mask and discarded them in the bin. Walked out of the unit.

She tried to find relief in the atrium, but it was unlit and lonely. The chapel was likewise empty and offered no comfort. Anise dialed Boyd's cell, and only got a recording. So her feet finally found their way back to the unit.

But the place seemed more claustrophobic than ever before. A prison. Anise knew for certain she could not stay on the ward. Not tonight. She had to get away. To make this stop. All of it. She grabbed her knapsack and slipped past the nurses, pausing only to scribble a quick note and stick it on Mo's closed office door. A quotation from Frida Kahlo:

I hope the exit is joyful and I hope never to return.

chapter twenty-Two

The late summer night air, cool on her face, offered a fall promise.

Hands in her pockets, Anise crossed the hospital grounds and headed down the street towards the bridge. She could already spy the river, city lights reflected in its surface.

Maybe the bridge would be the place.

Her feet padded the pavement. She thought back to when she was a little girl. Dressed beautifully. Sitting pretty on Daddy's knee. Mother smiling benignly. Back when her mother seemed benign. How old had Anise been? Two or three. Ages ago. An eternity. Back in Never Never Land when it was all so simple. Like a little kid's life should be.

She was at the bridge now. Traffic was sparse and the few night drivers paid the slight figure of Anise little notice. She put one foot in front of the other and headed towards the centre.

When had it all changed? Sometime around Anise's tenth year, her mother grew talons and fangs. Her tongue turned venomous and her skin to frost. And her father seemed to shrink to miniature. Just about when Anise started to have opinions and a mind and a will of her own. She'd been ordered to listen. To control her emotions. To watch that mouth of hers. To swallow the discipline doled out like some sort of malodorous medicine.

Locked in her room. To bed without supper. How to feel worthless. And less. And less. Until and if only she could disappear.

Anise glanced up and realized she'd reached the other side of the bridge. So it wasn't to be here then. She trudged on.

Ducked into an all-night drugstore. Wandered the aisles past the laxatives. Along the row of banal greeting cards. Glanced over the collection of cheap and tawdry paperback novels. Tried to shield her eyes from the stacks of zillions of fashion magazines with the skeletal celebrities and models grinning mockery out at her. 50 Days to a Slimmer You. Lose That Back Fat. Cellulite: Your No. 1 Enemy. It was enough to make her sick.

So Anise found the public washroom and peered hopefully inside. Several unflushed cigar shapes floated in the toilet water. She gagged and backed away.

And found instead the pain relievers in Aisle E. Chose the highest dosage with 10% more bonus pills. Grabbed a bottle of skim milk and a package of Ladylegs disposable razors. Paid at the till and left the store.

The evening breeze was chilly. She shivered. Then stuffing her purchases in her knapsack, continued on her nowhere journey. Downwards.

This time Anise headed towards the park. Maybe it wasn't safe, but then maybe that's what she was looking for. Someone else to do her in.

But the park was deserted. No ne'er-do-wells lurking in the shadows. Anise sat on a bench in a beam from the streetlamp, near the bronze statue of wise old Emily Murphy. She was a great fan of the woman and the Famous Five who'd worked so hard to have Canadian women legally declared as persons. To eventually earn the right to vote.

"Well, I won't live to exercise that right." She didn't much feel like a person anyway. Anise looked across the river along the route she had come. Scrounged around in her knapsack for her iPod. But Boyd had made her erase all the morose and tormented songs of her collection. She selected Sia. And opened the package of razors.

This was as good a place as any. And this time the cut would be deep enough. To cut out for good. She'd take the pills, too. Either way, by morning Anise wouldn't be. Anymore.

Only seventeen and so tired. Of this struggle. Of all this hurt. Life was full of hurting people. Wasn't she surrounded by them everyday? Wasn't she living proof?

One less person on the overpopulated planet. Who would notice?

Boyd.

His name snuck into her consciousness. But what good was she to Boyd? She needed him more than he needed her. What was she but a burden? Besides he had his own stuff to work out. She was a weight around his neck. In the end, her ending might be the saving of him.

But it hurt to think that. It hurt to think about him.

Maybe she could reach him. Just to say goodbye. Anise pulled out her phone and speed-dialed his number. But all she got was his voice mail. Again. She'd leave him a note explaining. He'd understand. Boyd had been on this dark shore himself. And pulled back from the darkness.

Well, Anise just wasn't that strong.

She fished out her notebook and ripped out a page. But words failed her. She sketched a flower. Flicked her pen. Finally, she could think of nothing except:

Dear Boyd,

I'm...sorry.
    Love,
        Anise

It wasn't enough, she knew. But it was all she had.

Anise opened the milk and took a swig. She struggled with the childproof cap of the painkillers.

Pain. Killers. Kill the pain.

She thought of writing another note to her parents. Changed her mind. Everything she needed to tell them had already been said.

Who else? Only her brother. Would he ever recover to read her goodbye?

Marcel's cocky grin flooded into view. It was hard to resist smiling back at the image. She let her memories spin in reverse. Before the fights with the parents. Back to the innocence. Brother and sister, together at the lake. Diving off the wooden boat dock. Marcel playing Jaws in the murky water. Reading comics by flashlight in the darkness of the summer cottage. Racing bikes up and down the street. Marcel in the lead, taking stupid risks off ramps and over obstacles, breaking his arm not once but three times. Even so he'd always seemed immune to real danger.

Until...

Anise let one tear fall. Just one. But stubbornly another fell. And another. And suddenly she was curled up on the park bench sobbing for all this loss. This grief. The real possibility that Marcel might die. And she might never have the chance to say goodbye. Or tell him that she loved him, despite everything.

"Hey, kid," a velvet voice came out of the darkness. "Are-are you ok?"

She raised her head and through her snot and misery, managed to nod at the young man on a bicycle who had stopped to check on her.

"Can I call someone for you?"

"N-no, thanks. That's ok. I've got my cellphone on me."

"You sure?" His helmet gleamed in the street light.

"Y-yeah."

Then, as if the young stranger had invoked it, Anise's cellphone rang.

"H-hello?"

"Anise! Are you alright?"

"Hi, Mo."

"Where are you? Exactly!"

"At the park across the river. Sitting next to Emily Murphy. Talking to a guy on a bike."

The bicycle Samaritan smiled then and saluted Anise. He drove off down the path.

"Fran found your note on my office door and called me at home. She's in a panic. We both are!"

Anise sniffled.

"You're crying."

"Very observant, Mo."

"It's ok to cry, Anise. It's important to feel."

"I know. You've told me about a hundred thousand times."

"Have you got a plan, Anise?"

"I did."

"Past tense." Mo sounded relieved.

"Yeah, I guess."

"I heard about your brother," Mo paused. "It's not your fault. His overdose had nothing to do with you, Anise. That's Marcel's to own. Not yours."

"I-I know."

"Good. Now listen up! You are a very important person in this world."

Anise glanced up at Emily Murphy. "Yeah?"

"To lots of people. Like me. And Fran. And Boyd. And very possibly thousands of, as yet, undiscovered others. You and I are working hard on helping you to find your way through this dark tunnel."

"I'm trying, Mo. But it's so hard. And it hurts so much." Anise's voice broke into a bawl.

"'Course it hurts. Being born hurts like hell, Anise. But that's what you're going through. The process of being reborn."

"I hate your metaphors, Mo."

"Too damn bad! I hate that you can't find enough love for yourself. I hate that you'd rather starve to death than live. Rather cut yourself up and off than embrace life."

"Are you angry at me, Mo?" Anise felt scared.

"No, Anise. I'm angry at your disorder. At the culture that makes it possible and promotes it. I'm angry that at seventeen you're so full of hurt you hope to die."

"I-I don't. Hope to. Want to. Die."

Mo heaved a huge sigh. "Good. Then let's get you back to the hospital where it's warm and safe."

Asylum. But by now Anise knew that the word had another meaning. A secure place of shelter or refuge. Sanctuary. 4-Psych-O.

"I'll come and pick you up."

"No thanks, Mo. If it's ok with you. I brought myself this far. I'd like to make it back on my own. Please."

"It's too far and too late to walk back, Anise. It's no problem for me to hop in my car..."

"Really, Mo."

There was momentary silence on the line as Mo considered her options. "Are you sure you can make the return safely, on your own?"

"I've got a bus pass, a brain and a heartbeat. Yeah. I'm sure."

Chapter Twenty-three

Anise's Tips for Anise:
1. Take one step. Then another.
2. Listen to music.
3. Sometimes make deliberate mistakes. Perfection is an illusion.
4. Forgive yourself for mistakes. Move on.
5. Get outside and look at the sky. Roll in the leaves. Or the snow. Touch something green and living every day.
6. Breathe.
7. Role play difficult situations (like your upcoming job interview at the Art Gallery Giftshop).
8. Turn for help when you need it.
9. It's ok to feel. Hurt. Angry. Confused. Scared. Happy. Love.

Anise reached for the kaleidoscope sitting on her bedside table. Boyd had given it to her that afternoon in the gazebo of the city park next to the Eliza P. Hospital. He'd returned from visiting his relatives and had rushed over to see Anise, when she confessed about her aborted suicide plot.

"I would have been very pissed, Anise, if you'd gone and done something stupid like offing yourself." Boyd stared moodily at the river valley just beginning to turn to autumn. "Particularly since I think I happen to be, you know, falling for you."

She turned a shy smile upon him. "Falling?"

"Yeah."

"Like these leaves?" Anise kicked idly at the first few that were swirling about their sneakers.

"Very funny." Boyd moved to turn away.

But Anise caught his arm, reached up and kissed him. "Boyd," she spoke softly, "I didn't do anything. I stopped myself. I got help."

Boyd sighed. "But what if you hadn't? Where would I be? And what about next time?"

Anise thought his words over. "The point is that I did. I made it through the crisis. And that makes me a little better prepared... for next time.

"I'm sorry I scared you. And I can't promise you anything, except that I'm trying my best here. That's all either of us can do."

He nodded soberly. "I guess." Then brightening, "Oh, I forgot." Boyd fished around in his jacket pocket. "I bought you this while I was away."

"A kaleidoscope?" She turned the cylindrical toy over in her hands. Put it up to her right eye and lifted her face skyward towards the sun. "I had one of these when I was a kid! Wow, that's so pretty!" Anise offered it to Boyd to take a look, but he guided the scope back to her eye.

"Just remember, Anise, the pattern always changes. You don't know what tomorrow's pattern is going to be. It could be equally as beautiful..."

"Or not," she murmured.

"Or even moreso."

"You're right," Anise breathed. "Breathtaking!" She lowered the kaleidoscope. "Thanks, Boyd. I love it!"

He grinned crookedly, clearly pleased with himself.

There was something very endearing about this bi-polar beanstalk. "You know, Boyd. I'm thinking of making like a leaf and falling for you, too."

"Let me know if you do," he pulled her close and breathed in the scent of her hair.

10. *There is strength in emoting. Tears are not a weakness.*

11. *Neither is taking your meds. Neither is reaching out to someone.*

12. *You are not weak. You are very strong.*

Anise knew the list sounded like those saccharine self-help books she and Marcel despised and mocked. But it was in her journal and no one need ever read it but her. Besides, Anise smirked inwardly, she was fond of saccharine, like all the other girls and women addicted to sweeteners on 4-Psych-O. And Marcel might never read her words again...

He was still in ICU. Still hooked up to machines and monitors beeping away mindlessly. Still in a coma. Her heart lurched to see him. To think of him. But none of it was in her control. None of Marcel's condition was her fault. She had surrendered to this fact. And one other: the future was uncertain for her brother.

But the future was uncertain for everyone, it seemed to Anise. Tomorrow would be a new pattern, but that was the only sure thing.

In a few short weeks, she would be returning to King Edward Academy for the Arts to begin a modified year. If all went well, she might be able to pick up the pace or go to summer or night school. But for now it was half-days of school with afternoons for homework or a part-time job. Anise aimed to build an art portfolio so that she could apply for a post-secondary art school in two years, perhaps The Emily Carr Institute of Art and Design on the West Coast.

Liz the social worker had worked with Mo to get Anise set up in a group home upon discharge from the hospital. Together they'd paid a visit and met the group home leader and the other young people living in the house. Rules were strict and curfew was firm, but until Anise could afford her own apartment, it was a safe transition place. She would learn basic living skills: cleaning, laundry, grocery shopping, and yes, even cooking.

She'd balked at none of this, until Liz, Dr. Z. and Mo insisted that she had to meet with her parents to discuss these new living arrangements and plans. If they agreed, it would be much easier and less expensive than going to court. Reluctantly, Anise agreed to the meeting. It was scheduled for 9 am tomorrow morning.

I am afraid of becoming my mother. But Mo says I am not her. I am learning to let myself feel. I am not shutting off from people. Or turning a cold shoulder to the world. Or on those I care about. I know it's a long journey, but at least I'm willing to take it. To learn how not to be her. My mother. If I am ever a mother.

I have other mentors. Other guides. Examples.

So I don't have to follow hers.

I want to be like myself.

I want to like myself.

•••••

Witless shifted uncomfortably in his expensive suit and on the pleather chair. Perfectly coifed and manicured, Loathed appeared indifferent and controlled. All was as Anise had imagined it.

Dr. Z. had already discussed her progress and the continuing course of treatment and maintenance. Now Liz and Mo were going over the details of Anise's new living arrangements.

"And you want us to sign these papers, in essence, signing our daughter over to the province for care?" Anise could almost see the frost fogging the air as her mother spoke.

"I hope you understand, Mrs. Jasmine-Luther, that this may be temporary." Mo cast a meaningful and silencing glance over at Anise. "We are all hoping for the least acrimonious course of action. In the interests of Anise's continued health and recovery."

From her designer clutch purse, Loathed pulled out a silver monogrammed pen. "Show me where to sign."

"Deirdre!" Witless protested.

But with a flourish, she had already signed her name and passed the document over to her husband. "Sign."

"No."

Deirdre raised an eyebrow. Dr. Z. coughed uncomfortably. Anise sat very still.

"I'd first like to talk to Anise in private. Please."

Liz, Mo and Dr. Z. stood to go immediately. "Of course."

"Deirdre. I'd like a moment alone with our daughter."

Her mother bristled. Her lips moved as though to make some parting icy retort. But she chose instead to leave abruptly and without comment.

The office was hushed. Anise looked anywhere but at her father.

"Anise, why? Why are you doing this?"

"I-I just can't live with you anymore."

"What have we done to you? Why do you hate us?"

"Dad," she struggled, "I don't hate you." Although secretly she knew that she came very close to feeling hatred for her mother. "I don't blame you, particularly, Dad. I just wish you'd stand up to her."

He stammered helplessly. "I can't... I don't want to sign this. I don't want to give you over to someone else. You're my daughter."

Finally, Anise looked at the man, shaken and near to tears, beside her. "Maybe," her voice was soft, "just maybe, I could be. If I live this way. Apart from you."

With a shaky hand, he drew forth his pen from his suit pocket.

"Maybe," she tried again as she watched him add his signature to the document, "we could make a real effort to finally get to know one another, Dad."

"What about your mother?"

"Some people should never be parents."

And though it was barely perceptible and as quickly suppressed, Anise thought she detected the barest of nods.

"Can I take you for lunch? Sometime soon?"

Anise smiled. "Ok."

"Is there anything you need?"

"I would like my weigh scale. And if I could... I'd like to borrow your camera."

"I'll bring them by on the weekend."

"Thanks."

"If you need money or... anything, come to me, Anise, will you?"

They stood and he hugged her awkwardly. She remembered the way he smelled, his expensive cologne.

"I will, Dad."

And then he was gone. The units were both gone. And Anise felt a curious mixture of freedom and regret.

•••••

The final day of Women Risking Art dawned. All the other participants had presented their pieces. Camilla the madwoman had grown increasingly animated in her spinning about the artroom. But despite her dizzying flights, her commentary had been very encouraging. She acknowledged the risks her students were taking. She applauded their integrity.

One woman who was quite lame and walked with a cane had created an installation piece consisting of ballerina shoes in various degrees of wear. Then she had danced, awkwardly but without her walking stick, to a piece by Tchaikovsky and to the rapt attention of her classmates.

Another woman, a Bosnian immigrant who spoke only broken English, shared the terrifying story of her flight from her country, as the class listened intently and studied the dismembered dolls legs, arms and heads collected in a plexiglass box as a testament to all she'd witnessed and lost.

Others explored, in thoughtful and risk-taking representations, the break-up of a marriage, the death of a child, the loss of a breast to cancer.

Anise had grown increasingly convinced that she had nothing nearly as noteworthy to share. Until finally the honesty of the women compelled her to likewise be honest.

Boyd helped her purchase nine pairs of inexpensive protective goggles and a sledge hammer from Canadian Tire. In secret she took a series of digital nude self-portraits. She photoshopped and modified one image into a distortion of her body. At the nearby printshop she printed this shot onto poster-sized paper.

Now she stood in the centre of the artroom circle around which sat her classmates and instructor. The photo of her nude self was exposed on the easel beside her. Her journal lay open upon the stool.

"I've been struggling with anorexia since I was thirteen. I'm seventeen. I can't look at my body without feeling disgust. I am always ashamed. Embarrassed. Self-conscious. Comparing myself to others. For me, it's a deadly game."

She read aloud:

Vogue

they can rebuild half a face
freeze up frown lines
suck out fat
cap the teeth
extend the hair
tuck the tummy
lift the brow
plump the lip
wax
exfoliate
expilate
exorcise the human
leave only the shell

any wonder why
midwestern
middleaged
matrons
pubescents and pre
obsess and cluck at
magazine photoshop dreams
cut themselves
off or up
puke misery
pilfer purgatives

swallow it all
and nothing else

"I measure myself by numbers. The grades I get. The width of my thigh. The calories I eat. Or don't eat. The numbers on this scale." She pointed to the expensive weigh scale her father had delivered from home, now placed also in the centre. "Especially the numbers on this scale."

She donned the goggles. The others did likewise.

"I'm so tired of measuring and weighing myself according to numbers."

And taking the sledge hammer in hand, raising it as high as her slight body would allow, she dropped it onto the glass surface of the state-of-the-art scale. Smashing again and again until it was completely, utterly shattered. Destroyed.

Panting, she removed her goggles. The art students did the same and applauded.

Camilla de Branscoville stood absolutely still.

final Words

I've come to the last page of my journal. It's filled up. Full. Satiated.

   Me, too.

   I listen to my friend play the piano. As I sketch in my book, E.D.'s hands seek out a melody at the black and white keys. Sometimes E.D. falters, but I don't care. We all sometimes falter. I know I do. At drawing. At writing. At life.

   E.D.'s music is a balm as I sit here in the sunlight.

   It feels good to bask in the sunlight. To see the light play with the hairs on my arms. To feel the warmth on my shoulder. Watch the gradations of shadow and light dance along the floor as clouds cover and uncover the sun's face.

   Shadow and light. Just like Ms Dobbin and Camilla coach me to use in pencil and charcoal drawings. Shadow and light. Chiaroscuro, a word that combines the Italian words for light and dark. Like the masters of Renaissance painting. Like in this Rachmaninoff piece E.D. is playing. Shadow and light.

GAIL SIDONIE SOBAT

Like in my own life. My own family. The parental units. My unmaternal mother. My unhappy inept father. My screw-up brother. And me. This illness. Getting well is like shadow and light, too. Lots of shadows. Too many. And even as they move away, they hover near my sun. But at least there is a sun. I thought for a very long time there wasn't. That I didn't deserve sunshine.

But. Maybe I do.

I deserve a little sun. Now and again.

For living through all of this. For making it.

Mo says so. So do Ms Dobbin and Mr. Rowe. E.D. says so, too. Zoe. And of course, Boyd.

Chiarascuro. Gradations of light and dark. Life and death. Living and the grave. The gravity of living. Yin and Yang.

I'm working hard on that balance.

Sunshine. Even though shadows hover.

What is the colour of hope? The colour of the sun.

I deserve a little.

On my arms. On my back. On my face.

On my words across this page.

If you or someone you know is struggling with an eating disorder or a pattern of self-injury, please seek help:

National Eating Disorder Information Centre:
www.nedic.ca 1-866-NEDIC-20 (1-800-633-4220)

Canadian Mental Health Association:
www.cmha.ca/bins/content_page.asp?cid=3-1036